BET OF THE BLACK BASTARD

BY DIYA SHAKOOR

BETRAYAL OF THE BLACK

COPYRIGHT ©2021 BY DIYA SHAKOOR

ALL RIGHTS RESERVED.

All rights reserved. No part of this publication may be reproduced, distributed or transmitted in any form, or by any means or system already in existence or hereafter invented. Any duplications of content must have written permission from author or his estate.

ISBN: 9798473815078

Library of Congress #:

Author: Diya F. Shakoor

Editing & Formatting: Diya F. Shakoor

Cover Artwork by Hard 2 Oppose Publishing LLC

Published by Hard 2 Oppose Publishing

TABLE OF CONTENTS

ACKNOWLEDGMENT

FOR THE READER

CHAPTER 1: CRIME SCENE

CHAPTER 2: THERAPY

CHAPTER 3: KEITH AND SHEKA KING

CHAPTER 4: RICH MAN'S PROBLEMS

CHAPTER 5: THERAPY SESSION 2

CHAPTER 6: AAYAN'S ARRIVAL

CHAPTER 7: USUAL BUSINESS

CHAPTER 8: VISITATION

CHAPTER 9: AAYAN DEPARTURE

CHAPTER 10: 1st STOP

CHAPTER 11: DEMANDS

CHAPTER 12: SLEEPING WITH THE ENEMY

CHAPTER 13: RANDY

CHAPTER 14: BUCK BREAKING

CHAPTER 15: HELL ON EARTH

CHAPTER 16: YURI

CHAPTER 17: FIX IT

CHAPTER 18: RECOVERY

CHAPTER 19: LIVE YOUR TRUTH

CHAPTER 20: HERB'S FUNERAL

CHAPTER 21: ONE MAN'S WEALTH

CHAPTER 22: AVERY

CHAPTER 23: BLACK BASTARD

CHAPTER 24: TORTURE

CHAPTER 25: MADAM B

CHAPTER 26: CLOSURE

EPILOGUE

FOR THE READER

Human Trafficking Defined:

The TVPA defines "severe forms of trafficking in persons" as:

- sex trafficking in which a commercial sex act is induced by force, fraud, or coercion, or in which the person induced to perform such an act has not attained 18 years of age; or

- the recruitment, harboring, transportation, provision, or obtaining of a person for labor or services, through the use of force, fraud, or coercion for the purpose of subjection to involuntary servitude, peonage, debt bondage, or slavery.

We live in a very dangerous world, a world of unknown truths for a lot of people. This fiction story is going to shed some light on the harsh reality that some children as young as three years old really live. The contents of this story may be appalling to some, but educational to others. Please be at mind this book is a fiction book but there will be nonfictional statical adaptations. I will share a few statistics for you before you indulge in the great read.

The issue of Human trafficking became a topic of public concern in the 1990s due, in part, to the fall of the former Soviet Union, the resulting migration flows, and the increasing concern about the growth of transnational criminal organizations operating globally. In 1994, the Department of State began to monitor human trafficking as part of the Department's Annual Country Reports on Human Rights Practices, focusing exclusively on sex trafficking of women and girls. As the understanding of human trafficking expanded, the U.S. government, in collaboration with NGOs, identified the need for specific legislation to address how traffickers operate and to provide the legal tools necessary to combat trafficking in persons in all its forms.

Human Trafficking was not statically tracked in the United States till 2000 when the Trafficking Victims Protection Act (TVPA) was passed. In 2001 the department of state established and presented the Trafficking in Persons Report (TIP Report) that began to account for missing people, traffickers, abduction strongholds and exploiters. As of December 2020, per the US State Department Trafficking in person report Traffickers are denying nearly 25 million people their fundamental right to freedom, forcing them to live enslaved and toil for their exploiter's profit.

This story is going to hit on the trauma bonding portion of the harsh reality human trafficking. In human trafficking cases, the relationship between victim and trafficker may involve trauma bonding, a phenomenon that is beginning to receive increased attention. In research on the topic, trauma bonding is commonly referred to as "Stockholm Syndrome," and the terms may be used interchangeably. However, there is no medical standard for diagnosis of either, or any agreed upon definition of trauma bonding. In addition, there is no definitive understanding of trauma bonding's prevalence within trafficking situations and not all trafficking victims experience it. Current research is mostly limited to the United States and focused almost exclusively on sex trafficking of women and girls. These research gaps create uncertainty regarding the prevalence and full impact of trauma bonding on all human trafficking victims globally.

-sources cited for this information 2020 Trafficking in Persons Report - United States Department of State

I hope you all enjoy and learn from Aayan's journey.

Acknowledgements

First and foremost, I want to thank the most high for seeing me on this journey that I am on and seeing me thru the high and lows of my life. I want to thank all of my supporters, family, friends and fans. I also want to thank all of my military family that I met throughout my arduous journey. There are a few people in particular that I would like to thank, my mother Victoria, Aunt Niecy, Zuwena, Antonia (Pooh), my brothers and sisters and my sons Christian and Diya Jr. Lastly. I want to say thank you to my first baby momma for putting me on child support. I had to find a way to hustle for money to eat… without your greed I would have never found myself. I hope everyone enjoys the read and I appreciate you purchasing or downloading the book.

"If you don't like it be the face of change."

Diya Shakoor

BETRAYAL OF THE BLACK BASTARD

CHAPTER 1
CRIME SCENE

Walking in the abandoned building that had been taped off as a crime scene. Yellow tape, police officers and EMT's are scattered all over the place trying to piece together what happened. The smell in the building was disgusting. The building smelled as if a mortuary refrigerator had stopped working. As the two crime scene detectives made their way into the main room, they were met by the first officers that arrived at the scene.

"Good evening gents... I have to warn you this scene is grizzly. There are two bodies, one body is located over by the wall with multiple gunshot wounds to the head and the other is strung up. The body that is hanging looks to have been tortured before he was murdered. They did some pretty inhumane things to him to say the least." said the Police Officer.

"Who discovered them?" said the Detective.

"A real estate agent that was coming to check on this commercial property to purchase."

"Take us to the bodies."

"I have to warn you... They look as if they have been here for weeks. The rats and decay have started to get to them."

"Nothing new with this job officer. Take me to them. Has the coroner been thru the bodies yet?"

"Yes sir."

Walking to the first body the detectives squat down and look at the body. They look at each other and agree that this murder wasn't a part of the plan. On the way to the second body that was strung up, their jaws dropped. They looked at each other slowly and looked back at the tortured body and demanded it be taken down immediately.

"He has been missing for weeks! Holy shit man do you guys know who this is!" yelled the Detective as he stared at the brutally tortured body.

CHAPTER 2
THERAPY

The truth of the matter is I don't know where to begin with this story. I have been thru a lot. Matter of fact a lot doesn't even scratch the surface of the atrocity of a life I have lived. Some may see me as a criminal, some see me as a multibillionaire mogul, some see me as bisexual because of the things I have endured while away. Shit some may even have the nerve to call me a faggot, but I pay them no mind. The things that I have endured in life no one can fathom. So where should I start this story...hmm with my name, I guess that's a start. I have gone by many different names over the long years of my life, nigger, boy, bitch, addict, dick sucker, pimp, hoe, traitor, survivor, but the most painful of all the names was bastard. The fact is I have lived all of these lives. It feels as if I am an immortal with all the lives I have lived in this short 25 years of life.

My name is Aayan, Aayan Petworth, you may know me as the CEO and founder of Petworth Pharmaceuticals and Petworth Promises Foundation. If you don't know me by these things by the end of my third therapy session you will. Everyone watched my rise to power and thought my life was peaches and cream, till the truth of my life was revealed. As soon as I try to let something go, there is always someone there to remind me that I was one of the many names that I went by in my short immortal feeling life. These people resurfacing are the reasons I am standing in this mirror looking at myself contemplating suicide before I leave out to go see my therapist. Some people can't leave things where they should stay... in the past.

Walking out of his large marble tiled bathroom towards his massive master bedroom in his penthouse suite that is located in downtown Manhattan, Aayan stood naked looking out of the open blinds admiring the bright sun piercing thru the clouds. He did this as a daily ritual before staring down at the city watching the people scurry along the busy streets like ants. From his view and his lifestyle everyone was ants. Aayan had endured so much pain and hurt in his life that he really didn't care for people and what they had going on, all he cared about was money and hiding the pain he had suffered.

Because of the things Aayan suffered in his journey he dressed as if he didn't have any money. Walking away from the window he reached into his rustic dresser and pulled out a fruit of the loom sweatsuit from Walmart. He figured if he dressed a certain way he could maintain a low profile in the public, meaning he could move without security and not worry about paparazzi stalking him. Sitting on the edge of his California king bed he turned the tv on to see his face plastered on CNN over a sexual harassment and assault accusation. As he started getting dressed all he could do is shake his head at the tv in disbelief about the things people would do for money. If they knew half of the things, he did for money they wouldn't be after him in this manner.

Walking towards his personal elevator he admired all of his custom arts from Rell, the artist Patrice and the Angelo Accardi collection. He valued these portraits heavily because they were all specially handcrafted for his liking. Before pressing the button on the elevator, he stared at his brown skin reflection in the elevator door and began to caress the permanent scars on his face before lowering his head to try to gain his composure. The lifestyle he portrayed he couldn't have a day where he was seen in the public without a smile on his face. That started from the time he pressed the button to leave his penthouse till the time he got back in after a long day of conducting business.

Today was a different day, today was the first day of a long overdue therapy session, the first of many to come. The therapist Aayan was going to see had come highly recommended and was praised for how she handled the confidentiality of all of her high dollar clients. Privacy and secrecy were things that Aayan didn't have the privilege of having in his life anymore. These sessions were what he needed in his life. It was hard for him to open up to people hence the reason he is still single, the reason he doesn't talk to family, and the reason he only has ten contacts in his cell phone. The contacts he had in his phone were all business partners, no family, no friends, no girlfriends, just business. He knew that was unhealthy that's why he sought out the help of a therapist.

    Pushing the button on the elevator, he turned his frown to a smile before he heard the ring just as the door opened. He was greeted by the elevator operator Mr. Jenkins. Mr. Jenkins was an old weary man roughly about 75 years old. He had been an elevator operator since the age of 16. It was something about the interaction with the people that kept him in the job his whole life. The conversations between Mr. Jenkins and Aayan usually set the pace for Aayan's day. Mr. Jenkins stories about civil right activism and effortless inspirational quotes made the day easy to start off with. Watching the door open Aayan smiled at Mr. Jenkins and pulled his mask up before being greeted.

    "Good morning Mr. Petworth."

    "Good morning Mr. Jenkins. You know you don't have to call me Mr. Petworth. I respect my elders and you are one of my favorites."

    "Mr. Petworth you earned the respect of being called Mr. You aren't one of these typical young boys out here with all their women, jewelry and ugly ego. You're a man Mr. Petworth."

    "I appreciate it Mr. Jenkins, what words of encouragement do you have for me today?" said Aayan as the elevator began to slow down for the lobby floor.

    "Take these things with you today on your journey Mr. Petworth, 'The greatest glory in living life is not in never falling, but in rising every time we fall'." said Mr. Jenkins as he opened the gate to the elevator for Aayan.

"Who said that? said Aayan as he stepped off and looked back at Mr. Jenkins with a curious smile on his face.

"The great Nelson Mandela. You have a good day and remember those words Mr. Petworth." said Mr. Jenkins while waving bye as the elevator doors closed.

Walking toward the exit of his building there were TV's with CNN playing all over the place with his face smeared all over it forcing him to pick up his pace to get outside to the blacked-out Tesla Cyber truck that was awaiting him. Aayan never really took the time to go get a license, he caught an uber or a lyft everywhere he went until he was rich enough to obtain a personal driver. He didn't like talking much in the car, so he hired a driver that understood that, his name was Avery. He was another older black man that Aayan could tell loved his job in service to other people. He knew exactly what Aayan wanted done he opened the door nodded his head and played music, that's all Aayan needed.

On the slow 10-block ride to therapy they vibed to the new Benny the Butcher album Plug Talk 2. Aayan wasn't your typical black man, he listened to classical music, soft rock, some country, jazz and African drum music, but when he did listen to rap it was either conscious rap with lyricism or underground rap. He wasn't into the gimmick rap, party songs and emo rap, that music had no substance and felt useless to him. Avery slowed down in front of the building where the therapist was located, he looked at Aayan in the rearview mirror, nodded his head, smiled and gave him a thumbs up. Avery knew that this was well needed in Aayan's life by the way that he carried himself. Slowly parking by the curve and turning his four-way lights on Avery exited the vehicle walked around and let Aayan out of the vehicle and shook his hand. Aayan began to walk towards the door he was tapped on the shoulder by Avery.

"Good luck Mr. Petworth." said Avery with a smile on his face.

"Thank you Avery. No luck needed I am just going to talk that's all." said Aayan before entering the building to find the therapist office.

Walking towards the front desk the receptionist spoke before he could even open his mouth.

"Right this way Mr. Petworth, Ms. Siler is expecting you." said the receptionist as she escorted Aayan down a long brightly lit hallway full of flowers and classical sculptures.

"This facility is exquisite. I have never seen such marvelous sculptures outside of a museum." said Aayan as he stopped to stare at a sculpture of a black boy crouching down and looking up as if he were looking to the heavens for help.

This sculpture stood out because there were many nights where Aayan felt this way. The boy in that sculpture in so many words was an exact representation of him. The pain on the boy's face was something you didn't need words to explain. The peering look into the sky was a desperate scream for help, well, that's the way Aayan interpreted it. He continued to stare at the sculpture thinking about what he endured in life, and it brought a tear to his eye. He didn't want to go into therapy sad already, seeing how it was the first session. He began to wipe his eyes with his sweatshirt before he was handed a few tissues from a short Caucasian woman with long blonde hair, hazel brown eyes with electrifying body features. She tried to hide her body in her business suit she had on, but certain curves can't be hidden no matter how much you try. This woman automatically commanded Aayan's attention.

"Good morning, Mr. Petworth. I see this sculpture is triggering for you, would you like it removed?" said Ms. Siler as she looked at the painful look on Aayan's face.

"Please you don't have to, I was just admiring the beauty of it that's all. If you don't mind me asking where did you get this?" said Aayan as he wiped his cheeks with the tissue.

"I will have the receptionist give you all of the information after the session. I am glad that you are here Mr. Petworth. This is a safe space. Just how you let those emotions out, you can let those out with me. I am here for you. If you are ready, you can follow me." said Ms. Siler as she started to turn away to guide Aayan to her office.

"You come highly recommended by a few of my colleagues. I can feel the nurturing demeanor and professionalism already." said Aayan while following Ms. Silers curvaceous body to her office.

Walking into the office the aura was set for therapy, there were pictures with motivational quotes all over the wall, a digital clock that reminded her of the time so she didn't run over, a cozy leather sofa for her clients to relax, a water machine that wad filled with water with cucumbers in it and a strawberry scented candle that was lit that made the room smell immaculate. The setting in the room automatically put Aayan at ease.

"Have a seat and get comfortable Mr. Petworth. Would you like something to drink?"

"Aayan, just call me Aayan."

"Aayan, would you like something to drink? I have water, tea, coffee and soda." said Ms. Siler as she stood next to the mini fridge by her framed autographed Barack Obama photo that she cherished.

"No thank you…"

"So, Aayan what brings you to therapy?"

Taking a deep breath Aayan began to think before he spoke. He examined the room one more time before he stared at Ms. Siler began.

"Well, you know who I am to say the least, but no one knows who I really am, not even me sometimes. I need a safe space to tell my story. I have been thru so much in my life that people don't know about and it's eating me alive. It makes me anti-social and it's unhealthy. I just want to tell my story without being judged. No one really knows my past and I really want to talk about it." said Aayan while rolling up the sleeves on his sweater.

"This is a safe space for you. There will not be any judgement here. What we discuss here will stay here, you are protected by the confidentiality clause that I am about to have you sign." said Ms. Siler as she handed Aayan the clipboard full of documents that needed his signature.

"Thank you for that. As you know I am a very high-profile individual so I can't share the information I am going to share with just anybody. People don't know anything about me they just know that I am rich. If people really knew the things that I have been thru and how I ascended to wealth, I would be perceived differently." said Aayan as he signed the documents.

"Aayan we will talk about everything that you want to talk about. How you came into the wealth that you did is a question that I had for you, but I'm sure you are going to share it all with me. Before we start, I want to say this to you, its respectable that you acknowledged that your behavior is unhealthy and needs to be addressed. The first step to fixing an issue is admitting there is one."

"I really need this. Thank you." said Aayan as he handed the signed documents back to Ms. Siler.

Sitting in the chair staring at the Barack Obama photo, Aayan closed his eyes and began to take deep breaths in and out in a calming manner. He knew the dark road he was about to journey in these therapy sessions was going to be rough, exhausting, emotionally draining and in some sense freeing. Aayan had been in a mental prison since his childhood, and he was ready for his release.

"Aayan, so before we begin what are you hoping to get from therapy?"

"Release... plain and simple just a release."

"Where would you like to start?"

"That's a very good question, maybe before I was born. You know every story has a back story... should I start there."

"You mean about your parents. I thought you didn't know who your parents were."

"I know who they are, I know where they live, I know that I have two siblings and I know they have no remorse for what they did to me." said Aayan as he clinched his fists together and popped his knuckles.

"How did you keep this a secret from the world?" said Ms. Siler as she sat back in the chair.

"Petworth isn't my real last name, it's King. Petworth is a name that I chose because of the things I went thru in life and how I was treated... like an animal. Essentially it only made sense to change my name to Petworth... There were dogs treated better than me." said Aayan as he sunk into the comfortable leather sofa.

"Have you tried contacting your parents?"

"No and I will tell you why in a second but let me tell you about them. This is information I remember from my youth. I had an investigator find out information about them before I was born. I needed to know what made them do the things they did."

"I am all ears Aayan, do share."

"Ok may I have some water before I begin?"

"Go for it, whatever you need to make yourself comfortable enough to open up to me."

Aayan stood slowly, stretched and walked over to the water machine. He looked out the corner of his eye to see Ms. Siler taking notes on her pad. It's as if she is documenting all of Aayan's movements, his demeanor and mannerisms. She is the best therapist in the city, so whatever she was doing he knew that it served a purpose in his healing process. Slowly filling up his clear cup with water, Aayan rotated his neck till it cracked loudly sending an echo across the room. He only cracked his neck in that manner when he knew things were about to get heavy.

"Sounds like you need to see a good chiropractor Aayan... I can recommend one to you."

"Look at you trying to put your friends on. You trying to share my wealth. You are getting enough money for five people from me." said Aayan in a joking manner before taking another sip of his water.

"Just trying to help you out, health is wealth. "

"I understand... well, let's begin shall we?" said Aayan before stretching one more time and plopping down on the sofa.

"Are you comfortable?"

"Can I lay down?"

"Whatever relaxes you enough to communicate effectively."

"Ok. You are sure that none of this will leak out? I don't want to go to jail."

"Unless you try to hurt yourself or you are planning to hurt someone the authorities will not be involved. You aren't planning on hurting yourself or anyone else, are you?"

"Hell no! I have too much to lose to be playing with people's lives and I damn sure aint taking mine."

"You'd be surprised how many rich people want to hurt people or commit suicide it's a very common thing."

"Well, I don't. I have hurt enough people in my life. Those days are gone and never coming back."

"Let's get on track and begin."

"We will but before we start, I want to know about you Ms. Siler. I am trusting you with my life story and I don't know anything about you besides your five-star ratings and high recommendations you come with. Who are you, before we get to know me?"

"What would you like to know without digging too deep in my personal life. I can't disclose too much of that because it may become a conflict of interest and it would violate patient-therapist confidentiality and that is a fundamental tenet of medical ethics." said Ms. Siler before opening the cabinet above her desk to pull out a full name plate.

"Hold on Tamika!"

"Yes, Tamika."

"Where the hell you from with that name. You are a blonde hair, hazel eyed white woman with a degree from Yale." said Aayan while staring at her nicely framed degrees hanging on the wall over his head.

"We all have a past, that's not what it's about, it's about where we're at and where we want to go."

"Let me find out you from the hood. Your husband probably black as the street itself. You know you white women love yall some dark ass men." said Aayan while covering his mouth to avoid spit flying out of his mouth from laughing so hard.

"I see you have jokes. No, I'm not from the hood. The love of my mother life was black, and she lost his baby. After they split up, she met my father, got married, birthed me and gave me the name that she was going to give her first child."

"Damn that's deep... I bet he was black as midnight too."

"My name is Ms. Siler not Mrs. Siler." said Tamika while smirking at Aayan.

"Oh, so no Seal looking man walking around your house. Interesting."

"That's enough of me sharing for today, it's your turn. Remember this is a safe space, you can let it all out."

"Ok..."

Aayan laid down and got comfortable again. He took a deep breath and thought about the last memory of his parents and how deceitful they were. He said their names Keith and Sheka King.

CHAPTER 3
KEITH AND SHEKA KING

"Aayan, are you ready?"

"Yes, I was just in thought, I didn't know where to start."

"Start where you feel like you need to."

"I don't want to go too far into detail or too far back so I will start from their high school days all the way up to my conception. Is that fair?" said Aayan while sitting up a little bit on the comfortable black sofa.

"Deal."

Where should I start? Ok so what I know of my parents before I was born, they were simple people I guess. They lived an adventurous life, but they were simple. A child was definitely not in the plan for them. They were neighbors growing up together and they knew that they would eventually be together forever, well, so I was told. As you can see the investigator I hired was good and did his research. Imagine being told about the wonderful life your parents have lived and are currently living without an ounce of remorse for what they did to their first-born child. As far as they know I am dead, and they haven't thought twice about it. I sit and wonder how my siblings were raised after me, and what their life was like. Too bad I will never know.

Let's go back to the mid 80's when times were simpler. The Ronald Reagan war on drugs had begun on inner city blacks, crack era was in full swing, police brutality against black people or super predators as they were called by the mainstream media was at an all-time high. Redlining was fully established in every major city, rap music had finally started really making a name for itself; black on black violence started to become the face of the community, unemployment and removal of jobs in the inner city began to decimate black families. The demonization of black people in the media and the oppression of the black communities due to systemic racism was consummate. Then there was the community my parents.

      My parents grew up in the suburbs of Washington DC, a small town called Baden. In the city of Baden during this time there was nothing but a gas station, a fire house and nature. It was a simple life away from all of the madness that they regularly witnessed on TV while watching the news with their parents. They lived a nice country life without the hassle of the inner city problems. They only knew chores, schoolwork, sport and family. All of my father's family lived on the same street, the only people they weren't related to was Sheka and her family. The two of them knowing they were going to be together wasn't something that was destined, it was lack of options. They were best friends, so why not be together forever.

      "You really did your research." said Tamika as she tapped her pen on the desk.

      "Family. I was told all they knew was family and how close knit everyone was. That's one of the most painful parts to me." said Aayan before turning his back to Tamika.

      "Are you ok?"

      "Yeah, just getting comfortable. Can you still hear me clearly?"

      "Yes, your voice carries well. Please continue."

      "Family... "

      My parents were star athletes at Fred Hampton High School of Cultural Development, my dad in basketball, my mother in swimming. They knew when they eventually had a child that they were going to have a superior athlete, but they winded up with me. Premature born, not fully developed diseased son. I will get into that later though. My parents received scholarship offers from every top school in the country. When I say they had options they had options, but they knew they wanted to attend school together, no matter where it was. All they knew is they wanted to be with and around each other for the rest of their lives. Imagine having that kind of love. I'm sure that is hard to find these days. The small tight knit neighborhood they were raised in was fully aware of the relationship between them and praised it. When I was five or six years old my grandfather would talk to me and point at them.

"Son you see that… that's young love. That's the goal to find your soulmate young and stay forever." said grandad Zeke as he stared at Keith and Sheka laughing at each other.

"What's a soulmate grandad."

"Your grandmother is my soulmate. She is my better half, she makes me complete. When you get older you will find your better half." said Zeke while glimpsing at the smile of his beautiful wife Berth Mae.

"Have you attempted to find a soulmate?" said Tamika.

"I thought everybody was my soulmate, going thru everything I went thru. A little piece of my soul was left with every deed I done. I don't think I have any soul left to share Tamika."

"Interesting. Continue." said Tamika as she jotted down notes.

"Ok."

Now my parents weren't perfect people they had their problems just like any other relationship, the difference is no matter what they knew they weren't leaving each other. Before I was born, I was briefed their days were filled with joy and happiness. During their senior year of high school, they had stints where they weren't speaking but worked it out. I'll start from the last stint when they weren't speaking. I think that's a good place to start up.

"Wherever you feel comfortable Aayan." said Tamika.

Walking down the hallway getting pats on his back in a celebratory manner from the students of Fred Hampton after scoring a season high 43 points against George Washington Prep and leading the school to its first ever regional title game the night before Keith could only think about making it to Sheka so he could talk to her. It had been a few days and she wasn't answering the window or the phone at home. Keith began to gather his thoughts as he got closer to her locker where she was leaned over having a conversation with a guidance counselor. He could tell she was disturbed by the conversation, so he knew he had to be there for her now more than ever. Standing to the side patiently waiting for the guidance counselor to finish talking, he started admiring her high yellow complexion, her petite 5'7 stature, her cornrowed hair and her jean jacket outfit that he knew she made herself. Watching the guidance counselor walk away he slowly approached her.

"Is everything ok Sheka?" said Keith as he reached out to touch her hand.

"Everything is fine, why are you acting like you care now?" said Sheka as she snatched her hand back.

"Because you know I do, so tell me what's wrong." said Keith as he reached to pick Sheka's lowered head.

"Keith, you know how we have always talked about going to college together and we would never be apart, well I think that may not happen." said Sheka as she put her head back down so Keith couldn't see her fighting tears.

"Why what happened? Did you not get accepted into Stanford?" said Keith with a concerned tone.

"I did get accepted. Because of my SAT scores they aren't offering a full scholarship anymore, I missed the mark for a full scholarship by 10 points. They would have to redshirt me my freshman year. I don't want that, and you know my parents can't afford to pay for school."

"Sheka we will figure this out, even if I have to take my talents to a different school. Wherever you go I will go."

"Thank you, Keith that's why I love you."

"I love you to Sheka. Which schools do you have full scholarship offers from? I need to know what my options are."

"Let's see ummm… Do you want the whole list?"

"The whole list! You are sitting here crying for what? Its kids in this school that are going to have to join the military, work a minimum wage job or worst sell drugs like we be seeing on TV. You have a whole list of options cmon Sheka."

"Do you want the list or not jerk!" said Sheka as she smiled while punching Keith in the arm in a playful manner.

"Ouch! Damn you strong… Let me hear the list of options. I know you have a lot, but you never shared this fully with me. Crazy self."

"Here is the list… Howard, Robert Morris, Houston, Western Kentucky, Towson, VCU, Richmond, Tennessee State, Baylor, North Dakota State, Appalachian State, Frostburg, Louisiana Tech, Virginia Tech, Tuskegee, UAB, UTEP, Central Connecticut, UNLV, Gonzaga…." said Sheka before she was cut off by Keith.

"Sheka stop… you have all these options and you're worried about Stanford. I know this isn't all of your choices, but I can get into any of these schools. You know that, right?"

"It's not about that, it's about getting a top notch education and competition. Stanford has that for us, well me more than you. The conference is trash in basketball." said Sheka in a joking manner.

"Shut up light bright looking like a bootleg Vanity." said Keith before pulling Sheka in for a hug.

"Well, you are my Bruce Leeroy Green." said Sheka as she swung her arms in a circle similar to Bruce Leeroy in The Last Dragon.

"You need to narrow it down to where you want to go so. Remember we are together forever no matter what."

"I will pick one by the end of the week and we can meet at your house with all of the family for my announcement."

"That sounds like a plan to me. You know prom right around the corner, have you and your mom finished this secret dress yall been working on."

"You will see the night of the prom, stop being pressed. C'mon we have to go I don't want to be late to class, I have never been tardy, I don't want to start now with so little grade school left."

"I'm just saying it's February but let's go baby." said Keith as he reached to carry her books.

"You may ask what this backstory has to do with my therapy session." said Aayan.

"I believe it's all going to tie together. I know you are telling me this back story for a reason. Trauma in life often starts way before us, it's genetic." said Tamika as she reached in her desk drawer for a piece of gum.

"I am and it's gonna hurt your soul once I tie it all together." said Aayan before he asked for a piece of gum.

"Here you go. Now please continue."

"Ok."

The stroll to class was short before they were interrupted by the basketball coach Mr. Witt. He was a short, overweight, older Caucasian man that didn't have one athletic bone in his body. The one thing he did know was coaching sports, he never played one in his life, but he could guide you thru anything involved with a football, basketball or baseball. Mr. Witt was a person Keith trusted like family. If he needed anything or had any questions, he could go to him. Waddling closer to Keith and Sheka he loudly spoke in his usual raspy voice.

"Hell of a game last night superstar. I wish I could keep you here for another year." said Mr. Witt while patting Keith on the back.

"Well, you know one of these days we will have a kid that's going to be just as athletic. Hopefully you can coach him or her like you did me. said Keith as he pulled Sheka in closer to kiss her on the forehead.

"I'll be retired by the time that child gets to me. Maybe I should start coaching younger children. I will think about that son."

"You should coach. You have a way of breaking things down so well that even our illiterate players can understand. I know you can teach some youngins. We have to go coach we can't be late."

"OK, have a good day superstar."

Watching them walk away Mr. Witt licked his lips and began to think about what their kid would look like and whispered under his breath. "I bet you two would have some very attractive children, I would definitely coach them the right way." He walked away slowly thinking about the idea of coaching children and it made him smile. The smile he possessed was of someone who knew he could change the world one kid at a time. He was such a respected pillar in the community, the thought of him mentoring kids would be unquestioned. He turned around walking backwards as he watched Keith and Sheka exchange a kiss and words.

"Have a good day today baby." said Keith.

"You too superstar." said Sheka in a giggling tone before she walked in the classroom.

"Tamika this picture I am painting for you doesn't even crack the surface of what's coming." said Aayan as he looked at his watch.

"I can only imagine. I saw you look at your watch. We are getting close to the end of the session so let's continue."

"OK, I will skip ahead. So, you know my dad missed the game winning shot in the regional finals and my mom chose Virginia Tech to attend."

"OK, pick up where you feel is suitable."

"OK."

The end of their senior year had come and the last things on the high school to do list was the prom and graduation. Both Keith and Sheka were prepared for what was next for them at Virginia Tech. Keith had received backlashed for abandoning his original college commitment, but he knew he was going wherever Sheka went. The day of the prom had finally come, and Keith was ready to see what Sheka had in store for him. She had done an excellent job keeping everything a secret. Sitting in his bedroom he looked at the tux sitting on the bed and hope it matched her fly.

"Boy are you dressed yet! That expensive ass limousine just pulled up!" yelled Zeke before he walked back into the living room where everyone on the block and distance family awaited.

"I'm getting dressed dad dang." said Keith as he turned up the cassette in his boombox stereo playing 'Choosey Lover' by the Isley Brothers.

He began to focus as he started getting dressed in his black and white tuxedo. Staring in the mirror at himself he grabbed his brush and began to gently stroke his hair confirming that he was the pretty boy everyone thought he was. At this moment he was sitting on top of the world, and it was only going to get better as the night went along. The drunk boisterous crowd in the living room began to drown out Keiths boombox speakers. He looked at the clock, smiled and thought about Sheka before he walked out the room and down the wooden steps with no banister. He had made the trip up and down the stairs so many times he never hit any of the family portraits on the brown wood colored wall. Keith walked into the living room where he was greeted by Zeke.

"There go my boy looking like one of The Temptations. This boy sharp aint he yall." said Zeke with joy before lifting his glass of moonshine and calling everyone to a toast.

"Cheers to a fine young man…he is one step closer to getting the hell out of my house for good. May the world be burdened with him now." said Zeke as he stumbled against the wall while everyone else lowered their glasses slowly.

"Shut up you drunk fool. Get your ass over there and sit down before you find yourself sleeping in the doghouse right where you belong for standing here talking out your ass." said Bertha Mae as she pushed Zeke towards his Redskins recliner.

"Thank you Ma. He always trying to ruin something."

"Don't thank me baby... you know he had one too many. You are looking outstanding honey. Go ahead and strike a pose for me so I can capture this moment."

Twirling around pointing his fingers at all of the flashing cameras he picked up the corsage and walked out their door where he saw the limo waiting. Heading over to meet Sheka for the prom, he was followed by the group of photo taking family members and neighbors. Inching his way up the steps not knowing what to expect when he seen Sheka he smiled, took a deep breath and knocked on the screen door.

Turning around smiling at the crowd one more time for photos he noticed everyone's jaws had dropped, and the flashes ceased. He slowly turned back around to see Sheka in a knee high dark blue, beaded, floral laced dress that fit her figure to the curve. Standing there speechless, Sheka had to break the silence.

"Do you have something for me?"

"I...I...Um...Ohh yeah I.." stuttered Keith as he tried to get his words out.

"Uh...Uh...Uh... give me my corsage boy." said Sheka while lifting her arm.

"You look so beautiful...How did I get so lucky?" said Keith as he put the corsage on her arm gracefully embracing all of the disposable camera and polaroid flashes.

They stood and took pictures together, with family and even with the limo driver. The night had just begun, and it felt as though it was going to last forever to Keith and Sheka. They left for the prom, where they wowed everyone as they walked in. They danced, partied and even had drinks at the prom. After the prom ended, they went to a party in Brandywine. This party was only for the coolest of the cool kids and they were indeed part of that crew. At this party there was the newest music, drugs, lots of alcohol and the sexual energy was immense. Like any other teen Keith and Sheka fell into the peer pressure of drugs and alcohol.

"Babe, I think we should go home. You have had too many and I think I have too." said Sheka as she placed her head on his chest.

"I agree. Let's go, but I have to use the bathroom first. I don't want to go home smelling like my dad."

"Ok I should probably do the same."

Walking into the bathroom together Keith turned the hot water on splashed his face and began to look at himself in the mirror. The solo staring was short lived before Sheka squeezed in close to share the mirror. They looked at each other in the mirror, smiled and slowly turned to look at each other.

"Hey beautiful." said Keith as he looked her in her eyes and pulled her closer to him.

"Hey." said Sheka as she reached back to lock the bathroom door.

'Let's get it on' by Marvin Gaye began to play setting the mood perfectly as Keith lifted Sheka head and gave her a long, luscious kiss on her lips. She started easing his jacket off as the tongue filled kisses began to create a moment of ecstasy for both of them. Slowly picking her up and putting her on the sink, Keith paused and stared at her.

"Are you sure? This is our first time."

"I'm sure. Are you sure?" said Sheka as she started undoing his belt.

Easing her fruit of a loom panties off, Keith guided himself slowly inside of Sheka moist, warm vagina. Taking it nice and slow he kissed her and tried not to stare at the uncomfortable looks of pain from her losing her virginity. The longer he inserted her the more satisfying it became to the both of them. He kissed her hard and long before a chill he never felt rushed thru his body, and he moaned in pleasure. They leaned into each other breathing heavily and began to laugh.

"Did you like it?" said Keith while holding Sheka.

"I like everything I do with you. I mean everything no matter what it is." said Sheka before looking down to see a half-erected penis covered in a combination of her juices and his.

Sitting up on the sofa and staring around the office before putting his head in his hands Aayan became silent. He then stood and turned his back, in attempt to stretch, he looked at his watch and began to speak in a low calming tone. Telling this back story was emotionally draining but it had to start somewhere, and he knew it.

"Tamika when she said no matter what it is, she meant it." said Aayan as he grabbed a cup of water.

"Aayan we are at a good stopping point for the day, we only have ten minutes left in our session. I think you telling this story is important to your healing and therapy process. Is there anything else you want to add before we close today's session?"

"No, I think we are good. I am just happy to tell my story finally. Same time in two days, right?"

"That's correct three times this week. Are you sure you are going to have time for that with you being who you are?"

"I'll be fine, I need this."

"Ok my assistant will see you out and I will see you in two days."

"I'm looking forward to it."

Getting up to walk towards the door Aayan's phone began to vibrate excessively from all of the alerts from CNN, Fox News, MSNBC, HLN, Yahoo, BBC, Al Jazeera, and The Black News Channel. The headline read 'Two More Victims come forward with accusation of sexual assault against billionaire Aayan Petworth'. Aayan wasn't big on watching the news, he actually hated it because of the false narratives, fear mongering, propaganda and lies that were consistently promoted to the docile masses in the world. Because of his level of success reached, he had to pay attention to the lies and trends for continued success. He depended on the docile masses especially being the CEO of a pharmaceutical company. His company just received five billion dollars from the government for Coronavirus vaccine production. In that aspect he needed the media to do its job pushing fear like it's supposed to.

Shaking his head, he hastily walked towards the door before he was stopped my Tamika.

"Aayan are you ok?"

"No, look at your phone. I am trending right now."

"Stay positive if you are innocent this will go away."

"Tamika, I don't even know these people." said Aayan while exiting the office.

Walking quickly down the hall he passed the desk clerk and stood in the lobby waiting on his driver to show up. He opened the article to read the accusations and began to wonder why his lawyer hadn't reached out to him yet. That thought made him close his phone and it was right on time. His driver pulled up and had signaled for him to come out.

"Boss, how was therapy today?"

"Good, I am just ready to get to the house at this point."

"I'll get you there as fast as I can. Just sit back and relax. You know I had a son some years ago. You remind me of him so much."

"Do I really? Thank you, Avery. Coming from you I know that is a compliment."

"Yeah, you can say that. Any music you want to hear."

"Can you play that new Conway the Machine for me?"

"Sure thing."

CHAPTER 4

RICH MAN'S PROBLEMS

Pulling up to the tower the streets were flooded with cameramen and reporters awaiting Aayan's arrival. Not only was the news presence heavy, but there were supporters and protesters outside with signs as well. Only thing Aayan could think about is how did these people found out where he resided. He lives a very private and cautious life because of his dark past. He never knew who would resurface with accusations that were real. Sitting in thought Aayan was interrupted by his driver.

"Sir, do you know what's going on?" said Avery as he slowed the vehicle down.

"Have you seen the news? Apparently two more people have come out and accused me of sexual assault." said Aayan as he pulled his phone out to open the news.

"Do you want me to take you to the back entrance?"

"They probably have that covered as well. Let's just keep driving, matter of fact let's take a trip out to Alexandria Bay. I need some quiet."

"You got it. I like the quiet out there." said Avery as he drove by the crowd.

"Thank you, I appreciate it." said Aayan before his jaw dropped reading the title of the article running on CNN.

"Are you ok your whole demeanor just changed? You know you can talk to good ole Avery."

"You will learn about it soon enough, it's all over the news."

"I don't watch the news, it's all lies. You know your truth, just make sure it's the truth."

"I like that saying. I think I'm going to have to borrow that."

"It's words you can have them as long as you share them." said Avery as he maneuvered thru traffic to get to highway 84.

"I will. Avery I will." said Aayan as he began to read the article.

Aayan's Accusations a Wealthy Mans Abuse of Power.

There have numerous accusations of sexual assault filed by women against Billionaire Aayan Petworth, but today we learn that 23-year-old Justin Reed and 24-year-old Sebastian Love are the latest to accuse him of sexual assault. The lawyer for the two men who have yet to appear publicly have gave their lawyer statements to give to the public. In the statement from the victim's attorney, they both stated on or around the week Feb 10th, 2020, at separate times they were drugged with date rape pills, physically abused and forcibly sodomized after meeting Mr.Petworth at a bar in Washington DC. The lawyer also went on to say that the two men are not speaking up for financial gain or to take advantage of the Me-Too Movement. They are speaking up because he was wrong, and they are looking for justice. He continues on by explaining how the two men haven't been able to date women and have been heavily involved in intense therapy in attempt to regain some normalcy in their lives.

CNN has tried to reach out to Mr. Petworth, but he hasn't been able to be reached at this time. There will be more to follow in this shocking story.

"Oh, this is some bulshit right here!" yelled Aayan while throwing his phone against the floor.

"Young man I don't think that was smart. If it's that bad your lawyer may try to contact you. You don't want it to look like you're guilty. Avoiding paparazzi is one thing, but avoiding the man who can clear this up is something different." said Avery as he merged onto the highway.

"You are right as always Avery. Man, I'm sorry to make you do all this driving. Can you turn around? I want to head to my lawyers office."

"You got it boss. You didn't make it this far in life making foolish, uncalculated decisions." said Avery as he veer to exit ramp without signaling, cutting an unmarked police car off.

Moving down the exit ramp the Black Ford Explorer began to trail Avery closely. As Avery began to slow the truck at the base of the exit the undercover truck turned on his dash lights prompting him to turn into the Texaco gas station. Sitting in the vehicle waiting on the police officer to approach Aayan leaned forward to pat Avery on the back.

"I guess it's just one of those days old friend." said Aayan before sinking into the backseat of the truck.

"No such thing... Everything happens for a reason."

Avery looked in the rearview mirror at the police officer in his car and at Aayan before reaching to the glove compartment for the registration. Opening the glove compartment the thud of a Desert Eagle hitting the floorboard shocked Aayan. Aayan looked out the window and closed his eyes because he already knew what the sound was. Avery looked over his shoulder and could see the clear frustration on Aayan's face and scrambled to push the weapon under the seat before the officer tapped on the driver side window. Aayan opened his eyes stared at Avery in disbelief and said one thing to him.

"I hope it's registered at least...you know New York isn't an open carry state."

Shaking his head, Avery rolled the window down and greeted the officer who had his flashlight beaming and a hand already on his pistol. The tension was extremely high. Avery began to wonder if the officer got a glimpse of the pistol that was pushed under the seat. The sweat beads began to run down the back of his neck from nervousness before the officer lowered his light allowing Avery to get a clear view of what the officer looked like. He was a tall stalky, Caucasian officer with a military style buzzcut. He looked like one of those types of officers that joined the force because he was bullied as a youngster. The people or public safety is never a priority to those kinds of officers. Staring at Avery with his hand on his gun still, the officer lifted his light again and started scanning the vehicle.

"Do you know why I stopped you boy?" said the officer with a country drawl.

"No sir... I don't." said Avery in a modest tone.

"Sir... you must have guns or drugs in this vehicle boy. My name isn't sir, it's Officer Kennedy and you will address me as so boy."

"Ok Officer Kennedy."

"I stopped you because you cut me off, you are driving erratically, and this truck looks too expensive for you to be driving boy. Are you a drug dealer or something? You know you can tell ole Officer Kennedy, I'll let you go."

"Officer Kennedy I am far from a drug dealer." said Aayan from the back seat.

"Wind this back window down boy so I can get a look at who just spoke to me."

"Ok." said Avery as he pressed the button for the window to lower.

"Oh, shit you are that billionaire rich faggot I seen on the TV today. Boy you sure do have it coming to your ass, but you probably will like that. Most of you modern niggers do like that homo stuff with your skinny jeans, fingernail polish and dress wearing. I don't know who you niggers think you are. I dont owe yall anything. If it were up to me, I would send you back to Africa or hang you in my front yard like an ugly black decoration."

Aayan wanted to snap, but he had to think about the weapon in the car. He also was smart enough to record the interaction in case the situation escalated out of control. Biting his tongue and looking away out the window, he began to take everything in that was just said to him. The names the policeman called him were names he was called repeatedly during all of his traumatic experiences. He stared at his reflection in the window and began to tear up thinking about all he endured from his childhood to his early adulthood. The pain he felt was surreal, it was something that money could not fix, no matter how wealthy he was. Money made things better physically, but emotionally and mentally money couldn't restore the empty feeling. His moment of sulking was interrupted when Avery commanded the attention back from the officer.

"Officer if you aren't giving me a ticket or a warning can we please leave, we have somewhere important to be." said Avery as he rolled the back window back up.

"Boy you will leave when I'm done with you. Give me that license and registration I am sure I'll be running you in for back child support, armed robbery or parole violation and that's going to make my night monkey." said Officer Kennedy as he snatched the license and insurance out of Avery's hand, tapped the roof of the truck and walked off.

"Avery something isn't sitting right with this situation."

"I feel the same way. With everything going on in the world with police and black people he is going out of his way to show us he doesn't care."

"I am recording everything so just maintain your bearings ok."

"I will, you just ensure you do the same. You don't need your name in the news for anything else." said Avery while looking at the officer thru the driver side mirror.

Aayan began to worry that the vehicle was going to be searched because of the type of officer they were dealing with. He began trying to slide his foot towards the weapon to ensure it was out of site. In doing so he began to think to himself about the officer and nudged Avery.

"Avery did you see a badge?"

"He had the light in my eye blinding me from seeing anything."

"Mine too. Something in my gut is not letting this situation sit well with me Avery." said Aayan as he looked over his shoulder to see Officer Kennedy exiting the vehicle.

"Are you recording" said Avery.

"Oh it's recording for sure." said Aayan before he was interrupted by a loud yell from Officer Kennedy.

"Who told you boys you can talk! Matter of fact Mr. Avery J. Chesterfield let's say you step out of the vehicle and come to the back. It looks like we have a problem." said Officer Kennedy as he slowly moved his hand back towards his gun.

"What kind of problem Officer? I don't have any tickets or warrants. I have never been arrested and I no children, so child support isn't a issue."

"You don't question me boy! GET OUT NOW! KEEP YOUR HANDS WHERE I CAN SEE THEM!" yelled Officer Kennedy while drawing his gun from his holster easing the barrel inside the window pushing it firmly against Avery's temple.

"Is this necessary?" said Avery while opening the door from the outside.

"OUT NOW BEFORE I PULL THIS GODDAMN TRIGGER!"

"Please hurry Avery I don't want anything bad to happen to you." said Aayan in a concerned tone.

Stepping out of the vehicle Officer Kennedy grabbed Avery by his arm keeping the gun to his head dragging him to the back of the vehicle. Aayan turned around to observe with his phone. He documented the whole situation that quickly spiraled out of control. Staring at the officer yell Avery with the gun to his head, he saw Avery stare at the outfit Officer Kennedy had on. Unknown to what made Avery react, but he knocked the gun away from his head and a skirmish between the two ensued making Aayan nervous. Not only was the gun flailing around and could be discharged at any moment, but Avery was in a physical confrontation with a police officer and there would be no way to protect his innocence if he were to be killed. He rolled the window down in disbelief and watched before he tried to intervene.

"Yall stop before someone gets hurt or killed!"

"Aayan he isn't a cop! I just heard his radio there are people on the way to try to kidnap you. Get in the driver seat and go." yelled Avery as he managed to wrestle the gun away.

"What!"

"GO!"

Attempting to climb thru the seats to get to the driver's seat Aayan heard four shots fired forcing him to look in the rearview mirror where he saw Avery running around to the driver's side to get back in the truck. Aayan in shock wedged in between the seats was brought back to reality by the yells of a bloody Avery jumping back into the truck.

"Move, Move, Move! Get back and hand me the desert eagle."

"Ok, ok." said Aayan while reaching under the seat for the weapon before he was slammed forward into the seat by Avery from hitting the breaks after being cut off by two all black escalades with tinted windows.

"What the fuck!" yelled Avery as he put the truck in reverse to back away from the men dismounting with assault rifles and pistols.

Trying to get away Avery backed over the body of the fake police officer angering the dismounted men who began to shoot their rifles at the driver side window and tires on the truck forcing Avery and Aayan to duck down while trying to get away. Not looking at the road Avery crashed the back end of the truck into a gas pump causing it to leak profusely on the ground. The shot began to halt from the gunmen when a voice that sounded familiar gave the command. It was one Aayan had heard in his past, one that he never wanted to hear again. Looking at Avery his concern began to grow about his life.

"Avery, are you ok?"

"I'm good I'm not hit."

"I have the gun."

"Give it to me and stay down. When they get closer, I will let the clip ride and get us out of here."

"Why can't we just leave?

"We have to slow them down. If we don't this situation is going to follow us."

"I have a feeling that it's going to follow me regardless. The question is who is it following me and why?"

"It doesn't matter now. Let's just make it thru this." said Avery as he peaked his head over the steering wheel to see how close they were.

Patiently waiting for the gunmen to get closer, Aayan listened to the voice again that sounded so familiar and heard something that would point him in the direction of who was after him.

"Vladmir, call Yuri and tell him we have the Black Bastard, and we are going to bring him in unharmed."

"Yuri? Who is that?" Aayan said to himself.

"Here we go Aayan stay down." said Avery as he shifted the truck into drive, and lifted up shooting in the direction of the approaching gunmen forcing them to get down on the ground.

The return of gunfire allowed Avery enough time to get the bullet riddled truck off of the gas pump spewing fuel in the air like a geyser. Speeding out of the parking lot he yelled at the Navigation system for directions to the nearest police station. Looking in the rearview mirror he saw Aayan looking over his shoulder out the back window watching the men run to get in their vehicles to pursue. He knew he had to get to the police station in an expeditious manner. As heavily armed as the men were the police would not stop them.

"Navigation in audible: Nearest police station 2.6 miles away."

"Boss what the hell is going on? Those men seem like they knew you for something other than being a wealthy man." said Avery as he weaved thru traffic doing 100 miles per hour.

"One of the voices sounded familiar but I don't know what is going on or why they wanted me."

"This wasn't a kidnapping of a rich man plot boss, they had intent for kidnapping you. They were calculated, precise and organized. What exactly did you do in your past life?" said Avery as he stared in the rearview mirror to ensure they weren't being followed.

"*Navigation in audible: In a quarter mile you have arrived at your destination on the right.*"

"That's a long story. That's why I am in therapy. I don't think they are following us." said Aayan as he turned around to see Avery staring at him in the rearview mirror.

"Whatever is going on. You need to figure it out! These guys don't seem like they are going to stop." said Avery as he parked in front of the police station door.

"I will figure it out."

"If they ask about this gun, I took it from the fake police officer."

"I got it."

Rushing into the police station, they both erratically screamed for help before they were greeted by the desk sergeant and five other officers standing at the front. The officers in confusion drew their weapons pleading for them to calm down, put their hands up and comply. Doing so in a hasty fashion the desk sergeant approached them and began asking questions.

"What is going? What's the emergency?" said the Desk Sergeant as he holstered his service weapon.

"We were just ambushed and shot at in an attempted kidnapping of Mr. Petworth." said Avery as he put his hands on his head.

"What are you talking about sir?"

"A fake police officer and two vehicles filled with heavily armed men just tried to kill me and kidnap him. Go outside and look at the truck, it is riddled with bullet holes."

"Oh, shit some action, whose truck is that outside?" said a Detective as he walked in the door.

"It's ours. We were assaulted at the gas station off of the highway." said Aayan.

"And yall are still alive? Well, that's a goddamn miracle that truck looks like Swiss cheese. You guys need to play the lotto tonight." said the Detective in a humorous tone.

"Look I don't know if these guys are going to follow us here but help us, please." said Aayan in a concerned tone.

"You fellas come on back here and let us get some statement and descriptions. You don't have to worry they would be brave to come up in here. This is the armory for the state of NY." said the Desk Sergeant as he escorted them to the back.

"I'll get a forensics team, a couple of officers and the on-call ambulance to go down there to check it out. You two just give the best statements you can, and be descriptive as possible." said the Detective.

"Thank you." said Avery and Aayan in unison.

After completing their statements for the police, Aayan and Avery sat in the lobby on an old wooden bench waiting for an armored Escalade to show up. Aayan didn't want to take any more chances till he could figure the situation out. Along with the armored escalade came a security detail that was going to stay by his side until further notice. The whole scenario made him sit back and think about who would want him this bad and why. This abduction attempt wasn't about the money, that he did know for sure. Staring at the blue concrete wall Aayan began to sweat heavily and gasp for air. Something about the big bricked blue wall triggered him into having a panic attack. Slowly grabbing his arm and leaning him back Avery whispered in his ear.

"Calm down young man. Breathe in and out nice and slow." said Avery as he started massaging Aayan's back.

"Is he ok?" said the Desk Sergeant while filling a paper cup with water for Aayan.

"I'll be fine, I just want to go home and rest."

Wiping the sweat off of his forehead and taking the water from the Desk Sergeant, he looked out the door to see two silver escalades pulling up in front of the police station. Cautious because of what just occured, Avery and Aayan stood up and moved behind the Desk Sergeant as he put his hand on his gun while four men walked up the steps to enter the building.

"How may I help you gentleman?" said the Desk Sergeant stopping the men in their tracks.

"How are you doing officer, I am Jason Morgan and I here to pick up Aayan Petworth. We were hired by Petworth Pharmaceuticals to perform duties as a security detail. He can verify who I am he received a code word that only we know."

Stepping from behind the officer Aayan stared at the men that were dressed in nice gray Armani suits and thick ballistic body armor. Looking at Avery and the Desk Sergeant he mumbled a sentence.

"I have been sitting in limbo too long without a championship. said Aayan.

"Not as long as the Redskins or the Wizards." said Jason while reaching to shake Aayan's hand.

"Nice to meet you Jason." said Aayan while shaking his hand.

"Nice to meet you as well. Sir we are here to get you home safely."

"Lets go please." said Aayan as he walked hastily towards the door.

"If we find any information, we will contact you Mr. Petworth!" yelled the Desk Sergeant.

Climbing in the back of the truck the adrenaline rushes that Avery and Aayan had quickly faded forcing both of them to fight sleep as the vehicle rolled out in a convoy style manner back towards Manhattan. Aayan knew as he drifted off that this wasn't going to be held from the media long. He already began thinking of setting up a press conference to discuss this amongst other things but not without the consent of his lawyer.

"Therapy is going to be fun in the next session." said Aayan as he giggled, before closing his eyes and going to sleep.

Pulling up to his home safely, Aayan woke up to see the crowd of paparazzi had dissipated. Staring out the window of the Escalade all he wanted to do was shower and climb in the bed. He knew not only was he going to attend therapy, but he had to speak with his lawyer and address the media. Stopping in front of the building the security detail surrounded Aayan and escorted him to the door before they were slowed by Avery's voice.

"What about me? What if they come after me?"

"I'll have a couple of guys go with you, but I know they don't want you." said Aayan while being shoved towards the door by the security detail.

"They saw my face, better safe than sorry." yelled Avery.

"You better not be late for work in the morning old man. I have a raise waiting on you for your valor."

"Shoot me a couple mil, some of them big booty women from Atlanta, an eight ball and a fifth of EJ and were solid." said Avery as he hysterically started laughing.

"AN EIGHT BALL!" yelled Aayan as he laughed out loud while looking over his shoulder at the vehicle with Avery in it rolling away.

CHAPTER 5 THERAPY SESSION 2

Waking up from a short restless night Aayan before his alarm went off at the usual 5am. Wiping his eyes trying to get them to adjust, he voice commanded his blinds to open letting the sunlight in. He quickly shifted his attention to his TV that he keeps on while he sleeps. There was a comfort from the low volume of Family Guy that helped him sleep soundly thru the night. Scrolling thru the channel guide for something to watch he abruptly stopped when he again saw his name scrolling on the news as a headline once again.

"Billionaire Aayan Petworth involved in shooting outside of New York City."

Scooting to the end of the bed Aayan turned the volume up so he could hear the broadcast. Staring at the TV they began to play the surveillance footage from the gas station where the incident took place. Struck with awe he began to wonder how this footage was leaked to the media this quickly. Was it the shooters? Was it the gas station clerk chasing clout? Was it the police station? At this point he just wanted to see what narrative was being painted as he began to listen to news anchor Gina Franks speak.

"In breaking news from an incident that took place just outside of New York City about 15 miles from Newburgh at a Texaco gas station. In this video you can see an apparent skirmish between Aayan Petworth's driver and what seems to be an undercover police officer before shots were fired and an ambush style attack took place on Aayan Petworth's vehicle. Yes, ladies and gentlemen this isn't a movie this is real footage of a gun attack. The motive and who is responsible for the attack is unknown. Aayan Petworth is said to be safe and sound with a heavy security presence for protection. The latest assassination attempt was not one of his characters with all of sexual allegations he has been accused of but a real attempt on his life. Is that a coincidence? Are the events tied together? Is he living a double life? Only time will tell in this story of Aayan Petworth. Now to Lucy with the weather." said Gina Franks as she picked her notes up and tapped them on the desk.

Turning the TV off and smiling only thing Aayan could think was today's therapy session was going to be fun. He had no intentions of talking about the previous night's incidents, if it came up. He knew he would deflect, he was already set on that. Closing his eyes having flashes of his violent rage filled past Aayan began to question who the armed men were and what they wanted. Besides questioning if he had enough security for them should they reappear. He questioned everything.

The sun began to peak brightly over all of the skyscrapers in the city illuminating Aayan's high priced condo. Not having much of an appetite he made his way to the shower to start getting ready to go to therapy. Letting the shower water warm he stood looking in the mirror having disturbing flash backs. It was something about running water that gave him the worst memories. Memories he wished he could erase, but some traumatic experiences can't be forgotten.

In the flashback

"Get your ass over here now boy, don't make me say it again!" yelled a fat white man in a German accent.

"Hey, you little niglet get the fuck back to work!" yelled a skinny muscular man in a Spanish accent.

"How much for the little nigger?" said an older man with an Australian accent.

"Stop crying and take it you black bastard." said a tall muscular white man in a Russian accent.

The flashback ended with a loud thunderous bang that quickly snapped Aayan back to reality. Before he delved too deep into his flashbacks the bang of a gun going off in his mind always snapped him back to reality.

He never understood what the bang meant. Was he supposed to commit suicide, was it his punishment for the things he had done, or was it a safety net for his sanity?

Shortly after his shower Aayan called down to his security detail to ensure they picked Avery up and they were ready to go. He did not want to be late to therapy today, though he knew that wasn't the priority in his life at the moment to other people, but to him it was. Getting dressed in his usual humble sweatsuit attire a buzz from the lobby came over his high-tech security system. Walking over and looking at the monitor, he saw Mr. Jenkin's friendly face and three men wearing black and grey trimmed Giorgio Armani suits who were heavily armed as if they were about to deploy to world war 3. Not recognizing anyone but Mr. Jenkins he called Jason to ensure they were his men.

"Good Morning, Jason, there are three men in my lobby dressed nice with an armory attached to them, are they yours?" said Aayan as he began to pace back and forth in front of the screen.

"Those are my men… Buzz them up."

"Tell them I just want Mr. Jenkins to come up and I still want Avery to drive."

"Sir, whatever makes you feel comfortable, we are here to provide you the best services available. Ill message them now."

"Thank you." said Aayan as he buzzed Mr. Jenkins up while looking at the three men who all looked down at theirs phones.

Patiently waiting on the elevator to come up, Aayan smiled. He looked forward to Mr. Jenkins wisdom of the day and bright smile. The elevator door opened and there he stood but not with his usual smile, it was one of concern, one that he never seen on his face before.

Knowing he was bothered, Aayan debated if sparking conversation was the thing to do. Before he could open his mouth, he was cut off.

"Mr. Petworth, I'm worried about you. I know it's none of my business but are you ok?" said Mr. Jenkins in a concerned tone as he stared in Aayan's young face.

"Good morning to you too, Mr. Jenkins."

"You know my wife wants me to quit this job because she believes you have some trouble brewing that may get me hurt or killed."

"Mr. Jenkins you are safe… please reassure your wife that you are safe."

"Are you sure? I hate when my ole lady is right. I will never hear the end of it even at my funeral. I can hear her now (I told your dumb ass to quit now look at you just funeral fresh as can be and still ugly.) I don't want that sir." said Mr. Jenkins and the elevator slowed for the lobby exit.

"I don't want that either and you know it. Can I have the inspiration quote for the day?"

"I'll give you a quote, but you need prayers."

"I'll take those too."

"But the Lord is faithful, and he will strengthen you and protect you from the evil one. Thats from Thessalonians 3:3. Just don't be the evil one." said Mr. Jenkins as he watched Aayan nod his head and walk off with the security detail.

Getting in the armored escalade Avery was comfortably perched behind the steering wheel as if the vehicle was his own personal truck. He had already put up his five air fresheners, set all of his favorite stations and filled his middle console full of candy, napkins and things people just don't need, almost as if he was a hoarder. There was a smile between the two and an awkward silence before Avery shifted the vehicle into drive and pulled off.

"What you feel like this morning?" said Aayan while looking out the ballistic window.

"Is this life now? I guess." said Avery as he vigilantly weaved thru traffic.

"No, it's not. I'll figure it out."

"I hope so." said Avery as he turned the radio on playing 'We Win' by Kirk Franklin and Lil Baby.

There was silence the rest of the trip. Pulling up to therapy they stared at each other nodded and Aayan exited being escorted by the security detail. Checking in, the receptionist didn't make Aayan wait, he was the priority for the day, Tamika made it clear that once he showed up to send him straight back to her office.

Walking slowly behind the quick paced receptionist he looked over his shoulder at his security detail and glimpsed at the statue that captured his attention on his last visit before he was interrupted by a sharply dressed Tamika. She had on a stunning gold tailored Hermes dress, one that came right above her knees. Her hair was in a neat ponytail and her glasses on her his face reminded him of the glasses Sarah Palen use to wear. She looked amazing.

"Come Mr. Petworth, I have a feeling this session is needed."

"Aayan, Tamika, Aayan."

"Sorry, Aayan." said Tamika as she walked in her office.

"What makes you say that?" said Aayan as he walked in the office and plopped down on the sofa.

"Let's see... Gun fights, attempted abduction, sexual assault allegations...if that video on the tv was accurate it's safe to say people died the other night. So, I am sure you need to talk today." said Tamika as she raised her eyebrow at Aayan and leaned back in her chair.

"What me...I have no idea what you are talking about. So where did we leave off a few days ago?"

"You are deflecting... Why?"

"Deflecting. What's that I'm just here to talk about my past to get it off of my chest."

"The incident the other night is the past as well. You don't have anything to say about it."

"I'm not at that point of my story yet, we can talk about that when I catch you up."

"It's your session. I was just ensuring there wasn't any trauma from these current situations that we have to work thru."

"There is... I'm just not there yet. We will make it to the texaco in due time." said Aayan before getting a cup of water.

"Ok let's start this session. How are you feeling today? Are you in any pain?" said Tamika as she began to take notes.

"I'm not in any pain... I feel regular... I guess good."

Observing Aayan's movements and paying attention to the inflection and deflections of his voice, Tamika knew he wasn't all the way together today, which was expected due to the day he dealt with less than 48 hours before this session. She did admire the fact that he even showed up.

"Now." said Aayan.

"Oh I'm sorry… please begin."

Leaning back and closing his eyes Aayan began to search his memory bank for the information from his youth and from what the private detective explained to him. A sudden cloud of darkness took over causing Aayan's mood to shift to a negative mind state. The darkness was as if he were alone in outer space just drifting with nowhere to go and no hope of rescue. The feeling of hopelessness, despair, heartache and pain is what brought him to therapy. In an angry tone Aayan spoke.

"OK I'm ready!"

CHAPTER 6
AAYAN'S ARRIVAL

"Tamika, I'll get straight to it today. I am going to start after my parents both graduated from Virginia Tech with honors and were living a great life. See I was never part of the plan, kids just weren't part of the plan at all, and we will get to that. When they had me it put a damper in their life. This I know for certain."

"Aayan how do you know?"

"I just know! So let me tell you the story." said Aayan as he closed his eyes.

"Ok, breathe and count down from ten before you start."

Inhaling and exhaling counting down from ten Aayan's anger and anxiety began to fade. He often tried to find a happy place in his memory to visit for relaxation, but he could not find one. The last good memory he could remember was the day's Keith and Sheka weren't arguing about taking care of him. Those days were far, few and close to none. As far back as he could remember in life, he could only see them mad at each other or hear them yelling. In Aayan's youth he thought that was what love looked like. Arguing, yelling, hitting walls, and furniture moving. Opening his eyes Aayan began to tell the story in a calm tone.

Keith and Sheka decided to stay in Virginia after graduating from Virginia Tech. They moved to Midlothian, a suburb of the Richmond area. This is where they would call home for the next couple of years. They lived in a quiet rural subdivision where they were one of three black couples in the neighborhood. They were looked at as a pariah to the neighborhood, but they didn't care, they were not moving. Life was great for Kings. They had married their sophomore year of college to solidify what they already knew they were going to do since they were young.

The comfortability they had grown accustomed to in life was from owning the best sports medicine and therapy business in the country, Trackball Therapy systems. They named it after the sports that helped them excel in life. Athletes traveled from all over the world to use the facilities and paid great money for it. Life was great for the Kings. They lived a life of traveling, partying and laughter. The two of them was the perfect couple, they had no worries. The two of them versus the world.

Leaving from the facility to head home one day Keith stopped at the travel agent's office to surprise Sheka with a seven-day trip to Egypt. He knew she loved all of the sporadic trips they went on and wanted to see her smile after they diffused from the day. Pulling into the driveway looking at the freshly cut lawn, the Ashley furniture on the porch and the shadow of Shekas attractive silhouette in the window made him smile. Exiting the vehicle and walking towards the door with the trip information, he turned around looked at the sky and spoke.

"Thank you so much for a beautiful life, a beautiful wife and a beautiful day." said Keith before he turned to walk in the door that was opened quietly while he was looking away.

"We need to talk." said Sheka in a mellow tone as she leaned back in the lazy boy in the sitting room.

"We sure do honey. I have a surprise for you, and I know you are going to love it." said Keith before looking to see the seriousness on Sheka's face.

"You go first."

"No baby you go first. Something is clearly bothering you."

Rocking in her chair and lifting her head she stared at Keith.

"I'm pregnant."

"BY WHO!" said Keith as he started to giggle.

"I'm serious, this isn't a laughing matter."

"I know it's not, I was trying to lighten the mood a bit. Baby I thought you were taking your birth control pills."

"I was Keith, I don't know how this happened. What are we going to do? This was not part of the plan right now."

"How many months are you?"

"If I could guess I would say going on three, I have an appointment tomorrow."

"Well, Sheka… we are married. It's not like this is out of wedlock, we are doing good for ourselves, I am sure we can afford to have a child. This isn't the end of the world baby. I thought you found out that you were dying or something. Come here." said Keith as he waved her over with his arms open.

"Parenthood wasn't in our plans right now." said Sheka as she put her head on his chest.

"Life isn't perfect, but you know what will be perfect, this seed that you are carrying. Our own little champion."

"I'm scared… I don't know how to be a mother."

"Sheka no woman does but they do it. If you want some lessons or support, we can move back to Maryland. The business is running itself we don't have to be down here." said Keith as he softly stroked her hair.

"That's a good idea." said Sheka while burrowing her head into his chest.

"I know what a real good idea, this trip to Egypt. You aren't too pregnant for that, are you?"

"I will know all about traveling after the doctor's appointment. It's at 9:15. I would like for you to be there."

"Baby is that even a question. I want to see how far along you are with my son."

"YOUR SON! How do you know it's not a girl?"

"My genes are too strong! You are carrying the next Dr. J in there. He is going to make that money, so we don't have to anymore. You watch what I tell you."

"Get off of me punk! You mean she is going to be the next Flo Jo. She is going to be fast as the wind in a tornado and brighter than the middle star in orions belts."

"Either way baby, we're going to have a champion. Do you feel better about this now? I know we can do it and think about it before we are 40, we will have a child on the way to college."

"You always find the brightness in everything."

Keith and Sheka left for the doctor the next morning and as Sheka expected she was 11 weeks pregnant. The Kings were about to have an addition to the family. Sitting in the office staring at the sonogram they were in awe. There was a subtle calming feeling that came over them. One of happiness, gratefulness and exuberance. Though there was as serene feeling Sheka felt while laying on the bed in the doctor's office, there was also still doubt in her mind about going thru with the pregnancy, but it was nearly too late for any other options and she didn't want to upset Keith with that conversation. The silence in the room was deafening and awkward. They stared at each other, at the sonogram and back each other before the doctors knocked on the door breaking the trance like moment.

"Mrs. King, you are good to go. I prescribed you some prenatal vitamins, some vitamin D and some medication for your Iron deficiency. Your iron and vitamin D levels are way below average, it may be from you not knowing you were pregnant." said the Doctor while writing out the prescription for the pharmacy.

"Is the baby in any danger due to those deficiency?" said Keith while rubbing Sheka's stomach.

"She will be fine, she isn't high risk. She just needs to take her meds."

"Ok... You hear that baby...our all-star is going to be good." Keith said in excitement.

"Yayyy." said Sheka in a sarcastic tone.

"Thanks doc... Let's get you home baby so you can kick your feet up and relax."

On the slow ride home down I-95 south Keith could clearly see that Sheka was bothered. He didn't want to dampen the mood by questioning if she wanted the baby or not. Instead, he smiled and turned the radio that was playing 'The Way You Make Me Feel' by Michael Jackson up. He began rubbing her stomach and singing the song. He knew his goofy behavior always made her laugh.

"At least he said you can still go to Egypt baby. Let's get out of here this weekend for a week... The getaway will be nice."

"You are right, let's do it."

Just as quick as they went on the vacation, it ended. Soon as they got back the reality of the world had donned on them again, work, a new child coming and responsibility. The fun they had on the vacation was one of the best and fulfilling vacations they had ever had. Fortunately, they had traveled all over the world in prior years. Unfortunately, the fun filled trip to Egypt would be the last overseas trip they would ever go on again, well at least for the next ten years.

Over the next month Keith handled all of the duties and some. He handled the business which included hiring a facility manager in their absence, Sheka's health needs and pregnancy wants, hiring a real estate agent to find a home in Maryland, putting their current home on the market and purchasing baby furniture. It was overwhelming but he knew what he had signed up for when they agreed to expand their family. In the days to come there would be little sleep for him but he didn't mind.

    Five and a half months into the pregnancy Sheka started experiencing difficulties due to her not taking her vitamin supplements and prenatal pills. She was doing this unbeknownst to Keith. She would intentionally flush the pills every morning when she went to take her showers and get ready for the day. Because of her blatant irresponsible behavior, she was a frequent at VCU Medical Center. During every visit they would add vitamin D and supplements to her IV bag. One of the nurses who was on duty most of the time she came to the hospital questioned if she even wanted the baby because of the way she was mistreating her health.

    Six and a half months into the pregnancy, Keith returned home from Maryland after finding a new home in Brandywine, close to Baden. He walked in the house and found Sheka laid across the kitchen floor with a full bottle of prenatal pills in her hand, and a mouth full of foam. She was wearing a jean jumper set that was soaked in blood in her vagina area. Rushing to her unconscious body he tapped her cheeks trying to wake her as he reached for the phone to call 911.

911 Operator: 911 What's the Emergency?

Keith: MY WIFE IS UNCONSCIOUS ON THE FLOOR! PLEASE HURRY! SHE IS PREGNANT!

911 Operator: Calm down sir... Is she breathing?

Keith: I DON'T KNOW PLEASE HURRY... SHE IS PREGNANT AND SHE IS BLEEDING FROM HER VAGINA AREA! PLEASE SHE IS UNCONSCIOUS!

> 911 Operator: Sir Calm down. What's your address so we can send help?
>
> Keith: JUST PLEASE GET SOMEONE HERE NOW! WE ARE ON ON ON UMMMM, PLEASE SEND SOMEONE! WE ARE 1134 HEXAGON PLACE! PLEASE SEND HELP.
>
> 911 Operator: Help is on the way! Sir Calm down and tell me if she is breathing. Is her chest rising and falling?
>
> Keith: YES! PLEASE HURRY! I DON'T WANT TO LOSE MY WIFE AND CHILD!

Just as quickly as he made the phone call the deafening sounds of ambulance sirens began to blare down the street towards their house. Keith sat in tears holding Sheka rocking back and forth as if she was a newborn baby. The violent knocks by the paramedics flustered him before he yelled!

"COME IN! PLEASE HELP MY WIFE AND CHILD!"

"We will do what we can sir. Please just ease back and let us handle it." said the Paramedic.

"PLEASE SAVE HER! MY FAMILY IS EVERYTHING TO ME!" yelled Keith as he stroked his head and paced back and forth.

"Sir, we need you to calm down. Your wife will be fine." said the Paramedic as he rolled Sheka on the gurney and adjusted the oxygen mask on her face.

Weaving in and out of traffic to keep up with the ambulance, Keith's tears made everything blurry. He could only think about his family and how much he would never let anything happen to them. Almost running into the back of a Toyota Camry, Keith brought his 1988 Cadillac Seville to a screeching holt causing the car to fish tale almost hitting the center guardrail. Wiping his eyes and collecting his thoughts he pulled off the side of the road easing back into traffic and calmly rolled till he got to the hospital.

Upon arrival Keith barely put his car in park before he jumped out and ran thru the emergency room doors yelling for Sheka, causing an uproar in the lobby. The desk receptionist called security to the front to control the situation.

"WHERE IS MY WIFE? I'M LOOKING FOR SHEKA KING!"

"Sir, calm down. We can't help you till you are." said the Security Guard.

Taking a deep breath, staring back and forth between the security guard and desk receptionist he calmly spoke.

"May I please see Sheka King? She was just brought here by ambulance after I found her unconscious at home." said Keith as he stood there trembling from the frustration of the situation.

"Mr. King she is in the maternity ward. Please have a seat and a doctor will be with you shortly."

"Is she ok?"

"She is fine, please have a seat. Someone will be with you shortly."

"Fine!"

"Thank you Mr. King."

After a thirty-minute wait in lobby pacing back and forth glimpsing at the 13-inch TV mounted on the wall playing "The Cosby Show" a doctor walked thru the double doors and called for Keith. He froze in place as a chill and cold sweat took over his body. Turning to walk towards the doctor his knees got weak and almost buckled causing Keith to stumble into a chair.

"How is Sheka? The baby?"

"Mr. King, Mrs. King is conscious and coherent. Everything is fine as far as her, but if we want to save your son we have to induce labor." said the Doctor while reading Sheka's chart.

"I'm having a son... do yall hear that I am having a son!" yelled Keith lifting his hands in the air in praise.

"Mr. King we are not out of the woods yet. She is only 28 weeks, and the baby hasn't fully developed so there may be complications or the baby maybe lost."

"No please don't let that happen."

"We will do what we can, but you are welcome to follow me to the back to see your wife."

"You should have led with that." said Keith pushing the double door open.

Walking down the hallway filled with women's screams and baby cries, Keith hoped he wasn't too late for the birth of his son. This wing of the hospital was so filled with joy and energy that you could feel it like a wall of water splashing in your face. Keith closed his eyes and embraced the feeling. It was that of new life and he loved it. Looking up at the flickering fluorescent light by the nurses station he heard a monotone voice say his name.

"Keith, is that you honey?"

Looking over his shoulder he'd seen a medicated Sheka laying in a bed with her feet lifted and nurses standing at her feet applying an epidural. Walking in the room kneeling by the bedside, he kissed her forehead and smiled.

"Baby, are you ok? You had me so worried."

"Honey I am so sorry."

"You didn't do anything wrong."

"I did Keith."

"You didn't baby… This is just something that happens to pregnant women."

"No Keith you don't understand… I never took the prenatal vitamins or any of the supplements that were prescribed to me. I have been to the doctor's numerous times behind your back over the months because of it. I'm so sorry honey." said Sheka as she started to tear up.

"Well baby, there is nothing we can do about that now. We are about to have our son, that's what is important. None of that stuff matters at the moment." said Keith wiping tears from her eyes and kissing her on the forehead.

She dozed off from the meds with Keith sitting in the uncomfortable hospital chair holding her hand with his head on the bed next to hers. The serene peace they felt knowing that she was alright. He was accepting and being by her side made it easy to rest but that was short lived. The heart rate monitor beeps became loud and rapid as Sheka let out a moan that woke Keith up.

"Baby, are you ok? What's wrong?"

"It's time to get the doctor, a nurse, somebody." said Sheka grimacing from the pressure she was feeling beneath the sheet covering her lower half.

"Going baby… Just hang in there." said Keith running out of the door towards the nurse's station.

"I think it's contractions, I could be in here for hours don't hurt yourself."

Scrambling to get back to Sheka's room with the doctor, they entered the doorway in surprise to see her sitting there with the baby in her hand. Because of how underdeveloped the premature child was he eased out without a real push. Sheka was only in labor for 10 minutes. She stared at the baby boy covered in blood with his umbilical cord still attached and immediately fell in love. Her maternal bond had kicked in and nothing could ever break that bond.

"His name is Aayan, Aayan King." said Sheka looking up at a teary-eyed Keith.

"Aayan it is baby."

"Well, we need baby Aayan Mrs. King if you will." said the Doctor while cutting the umbilical cord.

Not wanting to let him go. She watched the nurse put Aayan on the scale in awe that he only weighed 3 pounds 2 ounces. With him being born prematurely she knew it was going to be a while before baby Aayan made it home in her arms. The feeling of not wanting to be a mother had temporarily faded and she hoped that feeling never came back.

"Before we take him for shots and to the NICU, would either of you like to hold him one more time." said the Doctor.

"Go ahead Keith." said Sheka.

Picking the baby up off the cart and holding his small body in his arms Keith whispered to baby Aayan in a prayer type fashion.

"I love you little man. I will never ever let anything happen to you. EVER! You are my legacy, my everything, my son."

After eight hours of resting side by side in the hospital, Keith and Sheka made their way to the incubation room. They stood outside of the glass window looking at their son glowing under the light, holding each other, smiling and feeling complete. They stared at Aayan as he opened his beautiful brown almond shaped eyes to look at them. Almost as if he did it on purpose. His small, underdeveloped body warranted a longer than usual stay. The extended stay would give them more time to finish getting his room together and getting additional things a newborn needs.

Fading back to present day…Aayan paused, wiped the sweat from his head and neck with his sleeve. He looked up and watched as Tamika jotted down notes about the story she was just told. In his mind he thought she was trying to process the whole situation, maybe identify some triggering components of the story. Looking at the clock, reaching to get some water and stretching, he thought about the events from the other day. He knew he had to address that situation. Could it be his past coming back to haunt him? His mind ran rampant with possibilities.

"So, Tamika you see my whole existence was based on doubt."

"Are you sure this is how the story went?"

"Positive… Money has its perks, and I used my money well to learn this story."

"Family, never letting anything happen to me. That shit is a joke Tamika. So much happened to me! There is nothing my parents could say that would make me forgive them. I know my session is almost up so I will stop there."

"You have five more minutes."

"I also have other things to tend to, so we are at a good stopping point."

"Aayan your next appointment is on Friday. When you come, please bring a notepad and pens. We are going to do some exercises on stuck points and problematic thinking."

"Sounds good. I'll see you Friday."

Gathering his thoughts, Aayan walked out the door to an awaiting security detail that surrounded him. They ushered him out to his transport where a jolly Avery awaited to drive him to his next location.

"You ok boss?" said Avery watching Aayan get in the back of the vehicle thru the rearview mirror.

"I'm fine. I need to get to the lawyer's office and then to the board meeting scheduled at the my headquarters."

"Wherever you need to go."

"Thank you for being so good to me Avery."

"I have no choice, you pay me to good." said Avery hysterically laughing as he pulled off.

CHAPTER 7
USUAL BUSINESS

After a short six-block drive Aayan's convoy pulled up to his lawyer's office. The drive was quiet, no music, no conversation, just the silent hum of the heavy-duty escalade, horns honking in traffic and construction equipment. It's not often Aayan and Avery rode like this but it was an unspoken mutual feeling between them. In many ways they both were still trying to process the things from the eventful night. The fact that it happened had both of them on high alert. The distraction of music was unwanted.

"Avery, you know you are the closest thing to family I got." said Aayan as he marveled at the tall 60 story building where his lawyer's office was.

"You need to get out here and find you a woman. Start you a family... I can't be the only person that you find to be close like family."

"But you are."

"Well, I guess we're family then. Go handle the business with the lawyer so we can get you over to the next meeting."

"I'll see you in a little bit this shouldn't take long." said Aayan exiting the vehicle walking towards the high rise surrounded by security.

"I just want things to go back to regular, but I don't think that's ever going to happen." said Avery before the door was shut.

The atrium of the building was beautiful the ceiling is high and arching with paintings all over the ceiling. It looked as peaceful as the Sistine Chapel. The modern furniture gave the building a homely feel as if it were saying "Come inside, this is a safe space.". The tile on the floor was a beach tan color that immediately put you at ease walking thru the building. The architecture and presentation was immaculate. The location and everything just looked and felt like wealth, success and money. Safe to say that's why Aayan's lawyer chose it.

"What floor sir?" said the security guard as they stepped into clear windowed elevator.

"39." said Aayan as he turned around to admire the building interior thru the window while moving smoothly up the levels of the building.

"Do you need us to sweep the lawyers office?"

"He is no threat, and I should be in and out. Just wait for me outside the door."

"We will be waiting and ready to go sir."

Exiting the elevator, the office was directly to the left. It was the most basic door on the floor, but he also maintained the most basic office. The office was very spacious, roughly 2200 square feet in the corner of the building overlooking times square. He had all of this space and only thing he had in his office was a desk, his degree on the wall, an old sofa, a bookshelf with law books, a 13-inch wall mounted Vizio flat screen, a mini fridge and an old microwave from college. He kept it as simple as possible.

"All the money you make you can at least get a bigger TV." said Aayan smirking at his lawyer before sitting down.

"I live below my means, every humble servant of the Lord should, but look at the pot calling the kettle black. Look what you have on. Is that a Walmart fruit of the looms sweatsuit?" said the lawyer.

"How have you been Zack?" said Aayan reaching his hand out to greet.

"I should be asking you Aayan. You have more shit than an action movie going on. Sexual assault accusations, gun fights, stock losses, media talking trash about you and not to mention you can't a take shit without security. Are you ok?" said Zack Hill shaking Aayan's hand.

Zack Hill was a lean man standing at 6'2 about 190 pounds with blue eyes, brown hair and freckles. He was an LSU law graduate, he didn't quite finish at the top of his class, but he was great at his job, and no one could doubt that. When Zack wasn't handling high profile defense cases during the day, he was a playboy woman lover at night. Though his face looked odd, women could not resist him. It had to be his gift of gab and charm, for sure it wasn't his looks. Well money helped as well, though you would never know he had it unless you got to know him. He lived in a one-bedroom studio apartment in Harlem close to Garvey Park, he drove a Kia Optima and drunk 40oz beers when he wasn't out in the city.

"You know just an average day of a billionaire."

"Yeah, if you were Ironman or Batman and kind sir you are neither." said Zack as he began to laugh.

"Ok so what's the deal, tell me what's going on."

"You know you have four accusers now. One of them wants you in jail, the other three will go away for a price." said Zack as he leaned back in his chair to grab out two great value waters. "Do you want one?"

"Even though I live below my means, I don't live that low. That water is 70% chemicals and people just drink it all up."

"Most water is nowadays. Do… you… want… one?"

"No."

"Now listen the issue we have is that these accusers have actual dates and locations of where you were. Well two of them anyway. The others don't…We could just pay the three to make them go away and handle the last one with a settlement."

"Zack, I'm not paying these people. I don't know them. I don't know where they came from. Paying them would be admitting I did something wrong. I did nothing wrong. If we pay them more people like them will come out trying to get paid. If these people want war, let's give them war." said Aayan reaching for the great value water.

"Thought you didn't want the water."

"Shut up and get back to the lawyers of these self-proclaimed victims. Tell them we aren't paying a dime, we are going to court. The way surveillance set up these days we can pull the camera footage to prove I had no dealings with these people."

"You're the boss. I'll send the emails now. So what's the deal with all this Last Action Hero shit you have going on."

"I'm still trying to figure that out? They knew me I do know that much. Avery may need you, he shot people. We don't need that coming back to bite us at all."

"The footage shows it was self-defense so there shouldn't be a problem."

"But it is a problem Zack... since I reached the status I am at now there has never been anything of this manner to happen to me." said Aayan leaning back in his chair, looking over Zach's shoulder at the sun beaming off of all of the skyscrapers in the background.

"Hopefully this security detail is good and can't be compromised. I don't need my best customer in someone's trunk." said Zack as he flipped thru the channels on the small tv.

"They are good so far. I am getting my money's worth. The only real privacy I have is here, therapy and in my place. Even then, they are nearby."

"Hopefully whatever is going on works itself out."

"Hope so. Now get to work. I'm not paying you to sit here looking at me on TV."

They both looked at the TV that had CBS News playing. Turning up the volume they listened to one of Aayan's accusers Sebastian Love recollection of the trauma he alleged happened in Washington DC. He sat comfortably in the chair across from Gayle King in a nicely knitted brown Gucci suit with brown checkered color shoes to match. The spotlight from the camera gleamed off of his forehead as if he were covered in Vaseline. He stared at the camera with a look in his eye that was convincing enough to sway public opinion. Aayan wasn't concerned about public opinion, but Zack was. In high profile cases the court of public opinion means everything to the legal system.

Gayle: Good Morning Mr. Love, how are you today?

Sebastian: I'm doing well despite the circumstances.

Gayle: Let's get right to it shall we.

Sebastian: I'm ready when you are Ms. King.

Gayle: Where were you when this incident with Mr. Petworth happened.

Sebastian: I met him at a lobby bar at the intercontinental hotel in the DC Wharf area.

Gayle: How was he as a person?

Sebastian: He was mild mannered, just a regular guy having a few drinks and relaxing. I think he was more or less just looking for someone to converse with. Boy was I wrong! He started staring at me with a fire in his eyes as if I ignited the devil in his soul.

Gayle: Devil in his soul you say. I am sure that was terrifying.

Sebastian: That's the thing Ms. King it wasn't, it was comforting. I am by no means a homosexual, but he made me feel relaxed. He purchased me a drink at the bar and that was the last thing I remembered. I woke up in his room in bloody sheets, a sore ass, embarrassed, afraid and hungover. I didn't remember anything.

Gayle: How can you be sure it was him?

Sebastian: Who else could have took me to his room! HE RAPED ME! HE TOOK SOMETHING FROM ME THAT I NEVER WANTED TO GIVE AWAY. I FEEL LESS OF A MAN NOW!

"Man turn that bulshit off Zack! People have some very creative imaginations. I have never touched a man my entire life." said Aayan shaking his head at the small 13 in TV.

"You sure? He sounded really convincing." said Zack as he began to laugh at the TV.

"I got to go. I have a business meeting. Just fix this shit, make it go away." said Aayan stumbling over the edge of the chair walking towards the door where security waited.

The reality of the situation is Aayan didn't know any of these accusers or where they came from. He found it kind of suspicious that all of them were in locations that only a small amount of people knew about. He began to wonder if it was tied to the shootout incident. His mind began to work at a rapid pace, but he knew he had to calm down and get his thoughts together for the meeting he had to attend.

Trailing his security back to the elevator Aayan positioned himself at the back of the elevator again so he could admire the atrium of the building. Looking up this time the sun shined thru a window that beamed perfectly on him almost as if it were a spotlight from God being shined. The light made him glow. There had to be a meaning behind it. Could it mean today was going to be a great business day? Did it mean he was going to figure out what was going on with the shooting incident? He was in a state of confusion but felt bliss at the same time. The light made him feel like everything was going to be alright. He began to hum 'Get By' by Talib Kweli. Security looked over their shoulder at him and smiled.

"What you know about that? You're too young and too rich to know about that kind of music." said Larry the security guard.

Larry was a massive man he played seven years in the NFL as an offensive lineman for the Washington Redskins well the Washington Football Team now. That's so dumb. He stood 6'8 and weighed 330 pounds. He was more muscle than fat and dark as a moonless night in the woods. He had dreads that almost made him look like the predator but was soft spoken as a child. He was the only security guard that spoke to Aayan besides Jason.

"You can never be too young to understand what good music is. You can say I have an ear for it."

"Ok I feel that. After the meeting are we taking you straight back to your place?"

"That's the plan… I don't want to place anyone's life in danger until we figure out what is going on. I need to know why people are after me."

"As long as we are here you are safe sir. We are the best in the business." said Larry while scanning the lobby as they moved towards the convoy of vehicles awaiting.

Hopping in the back of the vehicle, Avery looked up and smiled in the rearview mirror. Aayan smiled back but underneath his smile was pain. He hid all of the pain and anguish he was going thru under his smile. Avery knew there was pain on the inside, but Aayan would never let it out and talk to anyone. Avery asked about his wellbeing everyday but never got a real response. With everything going on he knew now was the time he needed the most support but didn't push to ask any unnecessary questions.

"Next stop the office boss."

"Yes, last piece of business for the day." said Aayan as he looked at the rainbows the early afternoon sun made on the ballistic windows.

"Do you want to go eat afterwards? I can take us to that one spot you like K Rico Steakhouse."

"No thanks... I don't think I should be parading around in the public right now. There is too much going on."

"Ok, well that does make sense. You can't live your life in fear though. We both know that. Life has to go on especially with all this security you have. Think about this you have OG triple OG me by your side." said Avery slowing down at the stop light one block from the Petworth building, laughing and looking down at his phone reading a text he just received.

"Got into one situation and now you think you the Black Panther out here. You are more Fred Hampton than T'challa. You need to worry about that text your wife just sent you instead of being a super hero. Oh, and we aren't going to slide past that eight-ball comment either." said Aayan as he laughed out loud.

    Something in the text disturbed Avery, because his whole demeanor changed. He got extremely quiet and continued to stare at the phone. He didn't respond to the message, he didn't make a call, he just stared at the phone. The message made him frown up like nothing Aayan had ever seen. Avery looked up at the green light and drove quickly down the last block parking directly in front of the Petworth building. Looking back down at the phone that sat in his lap, Aayan began to worry about what the message said. Attempting to be nosey he leaned forward trying to get a glimpse, but Avery moved the phone to his pocket. Sitting back in the chair he looked out the window at his amazing building.

    The building was a newer building in the Battery Park area of Manhattan. The building was 50 floors of solid concrete with his office being on the top floor and the board room being on the 49th. The floors from 13- 48 were his employees, labs, testing areas, patient holding areas for clinical trial volunteers and production areas. There weren't many windows on the building. It was a special request by Aayan that a gargoyle and an angel sat at the top corners of the building by the Petworth Building sign. His companies weren't the only businesses in the building. He leased out office space at a reduced rate to small black business on the first 12 floors of the building. It was his way of giving back to the community, even though he felt abandoned by it. His sense of community was far from one of a typical black young man.

    Scanning his key card at the elevator he and his security detail stepped on heading for the 49th floor where his five board members waited. They were five of the ten contacts he had in his phone, one was Avery, one was Zack, one the private eye he hired for info, one was an accountant and the last he had was Lester Wallace, another black billionaire who came into wealth in an unknown manner. Many say he got it selling drugs, with no proof. Others said he sold women, with no proof of that either.

 Walking into the boardroom with the beautiful 30-foot-long meeting table, an already lit projector and the five board members that were eating Krispy Kreme donuts and drinking orange juice waiting on Aayan. They stared at him and started clapping in a joking manner. He knew they had jokes, but they all had different personalities, completely different. The jokester of the group and the closest to Aayan was the COO Herb Lyons, they met at a juice bar years ago and a natural friendship took off before he knew Aayan was rich. He was a tall roughly 6'0, brown skin and a self-proclaimed ladies' man. Next Caze Horn, he had met him thru Herb. His business and finance acumen were amazing, he was the most important addition to Aayan's team. They next two were Bryan and Byron White the marketing and media strategy duo. They were twins from West Virginia that Aayan managed to finesse away from the competing Gene Corps Pharmaceuticals. Lastly there was Buckholt (Buck) Meter, he was the executive of pharmaceutical research and manufacturing. Without his scientific breakthroughs there would be no Petworth Pharmaceuticals. His research has contributed to the creation of medication that has cured HIV in the early stages, the cure of Parkinson disease and life extending medications for pancreatic cancer patients. His bright, highly educated and dedicated team are responsible for saving millions worldwide.

 "Bout damn time! You out here playing war games and shit! Got us in here waiting on you." said Herb sitting at the head of the table with his feet propped up.

 "Right this fool is a combination of Bill Cosby and Nick Fury. Get you some money and don't know how to act!" said Buck as he patted the table laughing out loud.

"More like a gay R. Kelly slash Dolomite. Out here taking people against their will and being all in the action." said Bryan.

"Trapped in the closet ass." said Byron.

"Caze, you don't have nothing to say. Everybody else got jokes." said Aayan as he sat next to Herb.

"Nawl not really... I mean everybody knew you had a weird life. I'm just waiting for you to show up in your batman costume." said Caze looking away and holding back a laugh.

Everyone laughed hysterically out loud. These were the moments that Aayan enjoyed. These were people that he truly trusted from a business aspect. He really didn't hang out much outside of work with them. He didn't want to mix business with pleasure to much.

"Shut up. I didn't hear from none of yall! Guess who would have lost their job if I lost my life. All of you clowns with the jokes in here. Now that's funny." said Aayan with a sarcastic laugh.

"Aww somebody pussy hurts." said Herb making a sarcastically sad looking face at Aayan.

"Start the meeting fool. Thank yall for lightening the mood, I needed the laugh." said Aayan with a smile on his face.

"Well truth be told Aayan everything is surging in the right direction. The Covid vaccine is ready to go, we don't have FDA approval, but we have the money from the government to push it out and that's what matters." said Herb.

"That's awesome. Buck how is the research coming on the diabetes cure?" said Aayan looking at the slide Buck pulled up.

"We can make all the cure we want. Until people take their health serious and stop eating every piece of the pig this will be an uphill battle especially with black folks. I have more directed the research to helping kids who are born with it. Let's give those without an option a chance."

"Buck, I understand that, but everyone deserves a chance to live as long as they can. Man, woman or child if we can cure it, we will. We aren't here to take advantage of people or judge them, we are here to cure them. We aren't like these other big pharma corps who don't believe in the cure only the treatment. We don't do that, we save lives… Let's put our best foot forward towards that."

"You are right Aayan. We will get on it."

"Herb things are looking good man. All of you guys keep up the good work. Caze, can you email this quarters financial reports and overhead expense cost. I think all of the hard-working staff members are due for a raise. Especially if that government check cleared."

"I'll get it to you today." said Caze.

"Alright fellas…I'll let yall get back to work. I have somethings I have to handle that doesn't involve sitting in here cracking jokes with yall all day. Keep up the good work."

"Ok Batman." said Caze.

"Tony Stark wanna be ass." said Herb.

"Jeffery Epstein rich weird sex fetish having ass." said Buck silencing the room.

"Woah, they said as a collective. That's a little too far now." Before they let out a loud yell of laughter. Aayan got up to leave smiling at the laughter at his expense. He really doesn't smile much so this was a much-needed experience for him with everything that has been going on.

"I'll shoot yall a message later on. Yall be good." said Aayan as he walked out the conference room giving Larry the head nod that it was time to go.

Running him down before he jumped on the elevator, Caze stopped Aayan. There was validity in what Aayan said in the meeting. If something were to happen to him then they would be ass out. He had no known will, he had no next of kin and he was 100% majority owner of the company. Legally what he said was absolutely correct.

"Aayan, we have to discuss you leaving someone in charge should anything happen to you."

"Have Zack draw up some documents. I just realized how that sounded coming out. I should have been had something in place. I'm out here thinking I'm going to live forever."

"Well, I took the initiative of already preparing the paperwork for you. All you have to do is sign it. I have it in my office. I have had it for some time… this is something that I have been meaning to talk to you about for some time now. After these recent events and with everything going on now is the time to talk about it."

"Well, I have to review it first. Can I do that?"

"What don't you trust me now?"

"It's not that it's just a good business practice of all people you should know that."

"Yeah, you're right. I will get them over to Zack." said Caze as he looked down at his phone reading a text he just received.

"Ok cool. Later man I can tell one of your thottys got your attention in your phone. Oh and tell them fools with the jokes to get back to work."

In the elevator ride down Aayan usually stopped on the lower floors to check on the small businesses, but today he chose not to. He chose to avoid crowds of people and go directly home. He didn't feel right walking into places of business with armed security guards like he was the president. In his mind that would have been excessive and unnecessary. Also being in the public eye just wasn't conducive to everything going on.

    Walking thru the lobby with his security guards surrounding him, Aayan looked around and admired what he built. The ring of the elevator, the movement of people even the tick tock of the huge clock hanging in the middle of the lobby made him smile but that was quickly saddened thinking about what he endured to get it. These kinds of mood swings were common for Aayan. He tried to be resilient and hunt the good stuff, but the good stuff always turned dark when he thought about his past.

    "Sir, are you ok?" said Larry.

    "I'm fine just in thought."

    "We all have those moments sir. Remember every storm has an eye, but it also has an ending."

    "Those are some wise words, Larry. I will keep that in mind. I look forward to having you around."

    "Anything I can do to help." said Larry opening the door to the convoy of vehicles waiting Aayan.

    Turning his head to speak Aayan saw two men approach as if they were entering the building as many people were. One of them pulled out a 7-inch blade and violently stabbed Larry in the neck four times instantly dropping him to his knees. Before the other two security guards could respond the second man stabbed Aayan in his side deep enough for half of his 6-inch blade to disappear. Security from the waiting vehicles scrambled after the two assailants while the two security guards administered aid to Aayan and a dying Larry.

Laying flat getting his wound treated, Aayan looked down and saw Avery scrambling towards him with his phone in his hand calling 911. Closing his eyes temporarily from the pain of the stab he looked over at a heavily bleeding Larry. The gurgles of the blood in his throat were sickening and scary. Turning away to avoid the graphic scene, Aayan looked up at Avery.

"Is the ambulance on the way?" said Aayan wincing in pain from the stab.

"On the way boss!"

"I have to find out what's going on Avery." said Aayan as he looked over at Larry staring in his eyes as the life left them.

He watched his chest rise and fall one last time before he stopped moving. The suffering for him was over and in many ways Aayan wanted it for himself as well. The guilt he was living with, the pain from the accusations, the attempts on his life, he just wanted it all to end. Avery kneeled down next to Aayan looking at the bloody wound.

"It doesn't look to deep. I don't think they were trying to kill you. I think they were sending a message."

"Avery I just want this shit to end already!"

"It feels like it's just beginning boss."

CHAPTER 8
VISITATION

Sitting on the edge of the hospital bed staring out of the narrow lightly tinted window on the 19th floor of the Earl (DMX) Simmons Memorial Hospital Aayan massaged the stitches he received late last evening to close his stab wound. None of his internal organs were touched as if the person who stabbed him strategically placed the wound. The hospital kept him overnight for observation. Staring into the sun cresting over the skyscrapers he closed his eyes and kept replaying the sight of Larry laying on the pavement taking his last breath. He now knew that this threat was a real and had to be figured out. Trying to wait till therapy to discuss his past, Aayan knew he had to start thinking about the people he crossed, injured or killed if he wanted to survive this ordeal. His thought process was interrupted by a light tap on the door.

"Mr. Petworth you have a couple of visitors."

"One at a time please, I don't want to be overwhelmed. There is only one person I want to talk today and thats my therapist. What time will I be released?" said Aayan laying back on his bed.

"I believe its Jason, Zack, Caze and I believe the last female said she was your therapist, Tamika." said the Nurse.

"Send her last... I need the most time with her. Can you send Jason in please?" angrily said Aayan.

Sitting in the quiet trying to control his emotions Aayan stared at the black TV screen. He didn't want to turn it on knowing that the media was going to spin a narrative about him and all of the attacks that he has been going thru. They couldn't have any real clue of what was going on because he didn't know. It's the blind leading the blind. The media had mastered the art of creating narrative, spinning stories, fear mongering and pandering. Aayan hated the fact that American people were so brainwashed by the media when 50% was opinion, 45% was a lie and only a mere 5%

was the truth. A gentle tap at the door made him shift his attention back to the matters at hand.

"Good morning Mr. Petworth. How are you feeling?" said Jason closing the door behind him.

"How the fuck do you think I feel Jason? I was stabbed, I WATCHED LARRY DIE AND I DON'T EVEN KNOW WHY I HAVE SECURITY! SO, YOU TELL ME HOW I SHOULD FEEL!" said Aayan emphatically while scooting towards the end of the bed.

"Sir, I understand your frustration. We will do everything we can to address your security needs. We will double down around the clock, and we have to relocate you to a safe house. Whoever is coordinating these attacks has to be close to you because they know your schedule."

"It feels that way, but the circle of people I have around me would never do anything like this." said Aayan as he looked over Jason shoulder thru the door to see Zack and Caze talking to each other and texting what seemed like an important response to a text they received simultaneously.

"Sir, all I'm saying is you have to be careful. Also something else transpired last night, but I think your lawyer said he was going to talk to you about it. Just understand we have to relocate you."

"If there is one more incident, I will sue you for breach of contract. I'm sure my money is longer than yours so get your shit together Jason for my sake and yours." said Aayan as he stared in Jason's face with a look of frustration.

"There will be no more issues sir. When you get out of here today, we have to get you moved."

"Ok, have a good day. Have the nurse send in Zack and Caze. I need to talk to them together."

"Will do. Sir we will fix this." said Jason as he signaled to the nurse for the next two for entry.

Walking in the door the jokes from Caze started immediately. Though it wasn't time for jokes, it did lighten the mood from the conversation with Jason. There was something off with Zack, you could see it written on his face.

"I am BATMAN!" yelled Caze startling everyone at the nurses station as he walked in Aayan's room.

"Shut up man you don't have any sense at all."

"How you feel?" Zack and Caze said collectively.

"It's not the worst thing to ever happen to me but I was stabbed."

"Because you are superhero at night. Someone has found out your true identity and wants you gone." said Caze.

"Shut up man! Did you get that paperwork you were talking to me about over to Zack yet?

"What paperwork?" said Zack with a lost look on his face.

"I assume that's a no. You were ready for me to sign it Caze, why haven't you sent it over yet?"

"My bad I got busy. Some of us really have to work out here. We aren't masked vigilantes that people want to kill."

"What paperwork?"

"Zack, it's just paperwork I had drawn up as a backup plan should something happen to Aayan. Like a power of attorney almost."

"A power of attorney for a top five fortune 500 company. No sir... you need to send that to me for review." said Zack.

"I'll get it to you for review. With everything going on we have to be responsible."

"Well, responsibly get it to my office for review. You know better than that Caze. All things legal come thru my office."

"I'll let yall sort it out. I just know it better be done right or I'll fire both of yall ass."

"We aint going nowhere, you love us too much." said Caze as he reached his arms open signaling for a hug.

"Get away from me playing. You know I just got stitched up."

"Unfortunately, Aayan there is more bad news coming from all of this. Whoever these people are they mean business. If it's the same people...."

"Get to it man stop procrastinating and talk." said Aayan cutting Zack off.

"Look your private vacation estate on South Padre Island was burglarized and burned down. The footage from inside the house was leaked online, well the last part of it. Before burning the house down, they put a written note in the camera that said "AAYAN WE ARE COMING YOU BLACK BASTARD!" said Zack as he looked down at a text he received.

"How could they know about that place? I didn't even purchase it in my name."

"Whoever this is, they are moving very organized and strategically. Professional to say the least." said Caze.

If they are targeting me, it won't be long before they are targeting all of you. I recommend everyone get security, especially you two, Buck, the twins, Herb and Avery. I'm sure they want Avery after killing one of their men." said Aayan as he winced in pain from having the conversation.

"What time are they letting you out of here?" said Zack.

"I'm leaving after my therapy session with Tamika. I'm paying for it, so I am using it. I can afford the quiet of the hospital because I sure don't know what's waiting for me outside of these doors." said Aayan as he started to gaze out window into the sky.

"Yeah, you really don't batman. I also really suggest you stay away from the news. They are dragging you." said Zack.

"Thanks for the heads up even though you know I don't watch that shit anyway. said Aayan as he looked over Caze shoulder to see Tamika conversing at the nurses station.

Zack followed Aayan's eyes to the nursing station immediately spotting Tamika. She was her typical classy self but in his eyes, she had the glow of a superstar. Zack had looked back at Aayan and shook his head.

"Now I know why your ass want to be in therapy so much."

"It's not like that man. I really need it."

"I need her... what's the deal with her?" said Zack.

"Shoot your shot man. It's strictly business between us. I'm not even interested like that. She here, you here, just do it."

"She is fine as hell." said Caze as he groped himself staring at her.

"Both of yall some creeps. Get out!" said Aayan while waving Tamika towards the room.

She walked into the room, and it was as if time stopped for all three men. The way she walked was as if she was walking on air, and the brown knee-high spaghetti

101

strapped dress commanded their attention. Entering the room, the scent of her perfume graced everyone sense of smell giving all three men goose bumps. Caze stood with his mouth open, Zack began to sweat and Aayan just stood cautiously to move the room chair close to the bed area for the scheduled session. She was coming to check on him but when she seen him move the chair Tamika knew what he wanted. She was not expecting him to want to conduct therapy, but she also understood that he had a lot to talk about. His past troubles are deeply rooted and needed to be addressed.

"Hey Tamika... I'm ready for my session." said Aayan as he sat at the edge of the bed.

"You sure... You have been going thru it this week. You don't want to take today off."

"Hi I'm Caze business operations manager of Petworth Pharmaceutical."

"Hi I'm Zack, Aayan's lawyer. My gracious you are beautiful." he said lifting her hand and kissing it.

"Good morning, I am Dr. Tamika Siler and I'm on the clock gentlemen if you will excuse us." Pulling her hand back slowly and moving towards the chair Aayan placed for her.

"Ooooo cold blooded." said Caze as he began to emphatically laugh looking down at a text that Aayan caught a glimpse of.

Text: When will he be released? We need to talk.

"Now that that's over with both of yall get to stepping." said Aayan in his Martin voice not really thinking much about the text.

"Before I leave yall to do what you do Tamika. Here is my card, make sure you use that number on there. It's my personal cell." said Caze while staring in her eyes.

"I'll think about it. "

"It's not a no, I'll take it."

"Yall be safe out there and Caze set up the security for everyone."

"Will do. Have a good session."

Exiting the room, they closed the door behind them. Tamika got up and closed the door blinds so no one could see in the room. The light shining thru the hospital window was perfect. The mood was set for the session, but this one felt different. Aayan and Tamika felt the energy.

"Where do you want to start today Aayan?"

"I feel like I should discuss everything today. I don't know if I will get a chance to speak to you again. People are trying to assassinate me."

"Do you want to talk about how that makes you feel?"

"No, I have other things on my mind I have to discuss first. "

"Ok we are going to have to eventually get to what's going on now."

"We will but for now. Let me talk please, and I need extended time today if you are free."

"I am. You can begin when you're ready."

"Thank you for taking the time out of your day for this."

"No problem. Let me grab my pen and pad."

"Today is going to be deep so you may want to grab some tissue for the next few hours." said Aayan before he pushed the button for the nurse.

"How may I help you Mr. Petworth?" said the nurse as she cracked the door open.

"Please can you bring me two bottles of water and please ensure that I am not interrupted by anyone over the next few hours."

"No problem. I will be right back with your water." said the nurse as she walked to the minifridge behind the counter at the nurse station.

Bringing the water back in the nurse put the lock on the door and the do not disturb light on at Aayan's request. This was about to be a long breakthrough session for him that was needed very much.

CHAPTER 9
AAYAN'S DEPARTURE

I still remember this particular birthday. This birthday was my ninth and the most special birthday. My other birthday was more like real kid's events, but not this one, I was going to my first theme park. My parents were taking me to Kings Dominion, and I looked forward to it. That's all I had talked about since my eighth birthday. It was time for a change. All of my birthdays in the previous years were just cake, ice cream, a cheap toy, my father drinking heavily and a miserable angry mother. Only time there was peace was when they were at my grandparents' house. My childhood as far as I could remember was filled with trauma. That's what they call it now, but back then it was regular life to me.

Shortly after Aayan's stay in the NICU, Keith and Sheka moved back to Maryland close to Baden as discussed. The move back was seamless, it was as if it were meant for them to move back to Maryland. The support of the family, the time they got to spend with each other and the stability of everything was perfect. The 3700 square foot, four-bedroom, three-bedroom house they settled in was perfect. The house was in a five-star school district, so they were prepared when it was eventually time for Aayan to go to school. The house was located in quiet residential neighborhood on a cul-de-sac. The family of three was perfect. Keith went back to the high school to help Mr. Witt coach basketball part time and Sheka took care of Aayan with the assistance of Keith and and both grandmothers.

Sheka still didn't grasp the concept of being a mother and was still unsure that she wanted to be a mother even though Aayan was here. The thoughts of motherhood often made her angry because of the drastic life changes that had to be made. She was sharing the love from her husband, something she had never done since they met. They stopped traveling completely, the romance in the relationship had all but faded away and being a stay-at-home mom wasn't part of her plan. Sitting in the wooden chair rocking back and forth Sheka would stare out the window for hours at a time daydreaming about things being the way they use to be. In her mind it got to the point in the daydream where she was about to hurt Aayan, but Keith always came home or walked in the room to snap her out of it. He never knew what she was thinking, he just knew she was disturbed. This went on for years. Eight years to be exact and it brought Keith and Sheka to a breaking point.

    Eight years of hardship in the relationship got worst when the business they worked so hard to build began to go bankrupt. The amount of clientele slowed down due to the competition in physical therapy, the cost of improvements in technology and staffing issues. Money that they usually invested into the business was now going to Aayan and all of his needs. Being born premature there were specific health care and medications that he had to maintain until his immune system was fully developed. The health care cost and the regular needs of a child began to consume all of the finances in the King household.

    Sitting at the table reviewing all of the overdue bills Sheka began to tear up. She looked at a young Aayan sitting in the living room watching Sesame Street and a sadness took over. In her mind the problems started with him, the child she never wanted. Even in his young innocence there was something inside of her that wanted to drown him in a bathtub so things could go back to the way they were before he was born. The thoughts of all of the traveling, freedom, intimacy and the business returning to its golden stature fueled those thoughts in her mind. Easing in the front door in an attempt to surprise Sheka and Aayan, Keith stood in the doorway staring at the tears Sheka was spewing all over the table.

    "Hey baby, what's on your mind? Are you Ok?" said Keith as he walked over and massaged Sheka's shoulders.

"Keith, I can't do this anymore." said Sheka wiping tears from her eyes while staring at Aayan.

"Do what Sheka?"

"The bills, medical expenses, the failing business, motherhood... I can't do this shit anymore. I want life to go back to the way it was before he got here."

"It's always something Sheka! It has always been something with you for the last eight years!" yelled Keith as he slammed his fist on the table.

"Fuck you Keith. I'm tired of all of this shit. I am tired of him, you, these bills, everything!" yelled Sheka as she got up to walk out.

"Don't you dare walk away! What the hell do you mean!" said Keith as he grabbed her by the arm stopping her from leaving the room.

"Can we give him up for adoption? That would be one less bill and it would help us catch up a little bit." said Sheka tilting her head towards Keith to get a look at his reaction.

"Sheka... That's not going to happen. His ninth birthday is coming up, how about you focus on that. Make sure we have everything set up for Kings Dominion. He keeps talking about this... I want it to be special for him."

"I know, I know. How can I forget his damn birthday." said Sheka in a sarcastic tone while storming up the stairs to the master bedroom.

"Make sure you clean yourself up, there is a basketball tournament at the school I am helping Mr. Witt coach tonight. I don't want you at the game looking depressed. SO PLEASE GET YOUR SHIT TOGETHER!" yelled Keith as he walked to go sit next to Aayan.

"Fuck that game and fuck you." whispered Sheka as she plopped down on the edge of the bed and stared in the mirror.

"Hey buddy how was your day today." said Keith as he lifted Aayan up to give him a hug.

"It was good daddy. Why is mommy sad? Is it because of me?"

"No son. Mommy just dealing with a lot and don't know how to handle it. She is fine though."

"Are you and mommy going to get a divorce? I don't want that." said Aayan as he hugged his dad.

"We aren't divorcing." said Sheka as she stood at the base of the stairs looking at Keith and Aayan sitting in the floor.

"You heard mommy. We are good. Now I need you to be a good boy and go upstairs and start getting ready. We are going to see my basketball team play and guess who's going to be there…"

"Mr. Witt!" yelled young Aayan as he hopped up and down.

"Now go get ready boy." said Keith as he watched Aayan sprint up the stairs.

Sitting on the edge of the hospital bed Aayan paused in his story and stared out the window. The stare was as if he had just seen a ghost. Tamilka sat quietly. She still had no idea of where the story was going, it felt like senseless rambling, but she let him go. She looked away and looked back at Aayan as he began to speak again.

"Good ole Mr. Witt." said Aayan as a tear rolled down his cheek.

Mr. Witt admired Keith, Sheka and now Aayan. When he looked at Aayan he seen the perfect combination of Keith and Sheka. He himself never had any kids and for those reasons he took up coaching to groom and mentor kids. Mr. Witt did take up part time coaching for kids from ages 8-10. He learned they were more receptive at that age, but high school basketball would always be his love hence why he stayed coaching high school full time. Mr. Witt had an insatiable love for guiding male youth, particularly black male youth. He paid particular attention to the black male youth because the majority of them came from single mother homes and needed male mentorship. Mr. Witt was cherished in the community.

"Why is he important?" said Tamika as she looked up from her note pad.

"You are about to learn why, let me finish."

Later that evening the King family showed up to the high school gym where they were greeted by a jolly Mr. Witt. He had his typical small Coach Witt shirt with some tight khaki shorts that showed his full rotund shape. He was often the butt of jokes by the students, staff and opposing teams but his coaching was never laughed at. Before greeting Keith and Sheka he always spoke to Aayan. Mr. Witt loved the kids.

"Hi five little man. You look so much like both of your parents." said Mr. Witt lifting his hand up to greet young Aayan while wiping his forehead with his other hand.

"MR. WITTTTTT!" yelled Aayan as he jumped to give a high five.

"Sheka, how are you this evening?"

"Ready to lay down so can yall start the game. Please take Aayan with you and let him run around so he is worn out when it's time to go." said Sheka as she sat in the bleacher.

"Mr. Witt don't pay her no mind it's been a long day for her." said Keith as he walked over to the bench area holding Aayan's hand.

"Keith, make sure the guys are warm and ready. I'll be right back." said Mr. Witt as he looked over Keith's shoulder at Sheka walking out of the gym.

Sheka strolled slowly down the hallway going thru memory lane. There were trophies and medals in the cases for records she set in high school that still haven't been broken. Most of the newspaper clipping were laminated, framed and enshrined. She stood in front of the case with pictures of her and Keith at homecoming and began to tear up before she was interrupted.

"Are you ok Sheka? What's wrong?" said Mr. Witt massaging her on the back.

"Yeah I'm fine. Looking at these photos just takes me back to a simpler time, before the madness and motherhood. Life was fun and easy."

"Life is hard, but it's beautiful. Embrace the good instead wallowing in the bad." said Mr. Witt as the massage on Sheka's back became more aggressive.

"You having fun touching me like that Mr. Witt?"

"I'm sorry I thought it was relaxing you."

"I don't mind I haven't been touched like that in some time now."

"You should be touched like this all the time Sheka." said Mr. Witt as he touched her face and guided it to look at him.

"I'll let you touch more but I need something from you Mr. Witt."

"Anything."

After a conversation in the hallway Sheka and Mr. Witt walked back in the gym laughing and smiling. Seeing that made Keith smile. He hadn't seen a smile on her face in months. Keith knew Mr. Witt had a way with words that put everything in perspective no matter how difficult the situation was in life. Turning his focus back on the court he, watched Aayan get in the layup line like he was on the team. The basketball team loved Aayan. He served as a secondary mascot for the team with all of his cheering and interacting with the players.

Leaving the game Sheka was in a better mood. It was almost as if the dark cloud had lifted off of her. Walking to the car she seen Mr. Witt walking to his car, and she waived vigorously with excitement. Keith was perplexed about her newfound energy as he opened the door for her, but it didn't matter he was just glad she was happy. The ride home was pleasant, no arguing, no yelling, just the smooth tunes of the temptation and mellow conversation.

"Baby you seem happier. Mr. Witt really made you feel better," said Keith as he touched her leg.

"He did. I needed the pep talk. We will be alright." said Sheka massaging his hand with confidence.

"I know we will be. I know we are being tried in life right now, but things will get better."

"Keith first thing in the morning I am going to make all of the arrangements for our trip to Kings Dominion for Aayan's birthday."

"I like the sound of that. You know his birthday will be here before you know it."

The months flew by. It was a warm sunny morning. Keith and Sheka sat in the kitchen watching the weather forecast on Fox 5 on their nine-inch tv. Waiting on Aayan to wake up they worked in tandem to make all of his favorite breakfast food. There were heart shaped pancakes, eggs, crispy bacon, yogurt and apple juice. All of his favorites. Keith and Sheka smiled at each other. The months that have passed were peaceful and all about family. Laying everything on the table Keith and Sheka hugged, kissed and began to dance slowly to the beat of each other's hearts. Looking over Keith's shoulder blinded by the sunlight coming thru the blinds over the sink, Sheka watched a little silhouette form in the kitchen doorway.

"Good morning son. Happy Birthday!" said Sheka as she waved her hand over for him to dance with them.

"Happy Birthday son we made your favorite breakfast."

"I smelled it dad. That's what woke me up." said Aayan as he wiped the cold out of his eyes.

"Go ahead and eat Aayan, this is all for you."

"Can we pack it to go and head to Kings Dominion. Pleeeeaasssseeee."

"After breakfast Aayan you don't want to be out there in the heat on an empty stomach." said Keith.

"Ok dad."

The day was off to a perfect start. Breakfast was unlike anything Aayan had in recent memory. It was always cereal or oatmeal. In his mind this was going to be the best day of his life. Keith and Sheka held each other looking at him as he sat at the rustic kitchen table. The sunlight shined perfectly thru the blinds on Aayan making him glow like the golden child. The sound of the birds chirping in the morning created an ambience of peace. Quickly scarfing down his breakfast Aayan sprinted up the stairs with a big smile on his face.

Walking into his room he already had his outfit laid out as if he were preparing for the first day of school. His room was filled with posters of roller coasters, The Simpsons and The Smurfs. All of these things were his favorite things in the world. His obsession with roller coasters often confused Keith and Sheka because it was sudden. Sitting on the edge of the bed before getting dressed Aayan closed his eyes put his hands in the air and yelled "woohoo" pretending he was riding the rebel yell roller coaster. Keith and Sheka heard him and laughed hysterically.

"Go get ready baby. He is ready to go. There shouldn't be any traffic this early in the morning and we should be able to get good parking."

"Ok Keith… you going to clean the kitchen."

"I got it baby."

Scurring up the stairs Sheka ran in the master bedroom and closed the door. She stood staring in the mirror at herself pulling her hair back holding it with one hand while making sad faces. She opened the door slightly looked down the hallway to ensure Keith wasn't coming, ran to the housephone on the nightstand and made a call.

Sheka: We are leaving in twenty minutes.

Unknown Person: We are already here.

Sheka heard Keiths heavy feet walking up the stairs, so she hung up the phone and scrambled to the bathroom to turn the shower on. She looked in the mirror again before she dropped her robe to the floor. Looking at the stretch marks on her body she smirked at herself and made an evil grin before jumping in the shower. The water running down her body gave a sense of relief from the darkness she had felt brewing on the inside.

"Is there room for one more baby?" said Keith while looking thru the closet for an outfit.

"You know we don't have time for that. Not on the little man's day."

"You know I only need two minutes if that with your fine ass."

"Shut up and get in the shower." said Sheka as she walked out the bathroom wrapped in a towel.

The morning preparation went quickly for everyone and the trip to King Dominion was on its way. The car was filled with gifts for Aayan, a cooler full of water and juice, snacks and Aayan's favorite lemon pound cake for his birthday. During the whole hour and fifteen-minute drive Aayan rocked back and forth with excitement staring out the window at the trees and passing cars. Sheka looked back at Aayan and smiled before she asked him to play I SPY. Just as she asked him to spy something blue the Kings Dominion standing tall above the tree lines on I95 appeared as bright as the sun.

"I SPY KINGS DOMINION!" yelled Aayan as he began to frantically hop around in the backseat.

"Yay you win." said Keith and Sheka in tandem.

"Dad, Mom I can see the Rebel Yell from here. Can we go to that ride first?"

"We will get to it Aayan." said Keith as he made his way to the closet parking spot to the gate.

Sitting in the 1993 Chevy Caprice station wagon they rented for the road trip they ate and drank some of the food they packed. Aayan climbed out of the car stared thru the blinding sunlight at the Kings Dominion sign next to the park entrance. He turned around to see Keith and Sheka standing side by side holding a box labeled Happy Birthday. He screamed with joy and excitement and ran towards them snatching the box out of their hands.

"Can I open it now!"

"Sure, Aayan." said Keith as he put his arm around Sheka while she lifted up the polaroid camera.

Ripping the box open, throwing the wrapping everywhere Aayan pulled out a Simpsons t-shirt, a Nintendo Gameboy and a Super Mario Cartridge. He went ballistic in joy over his second gift with Kings Dominion being his first. Keith and Sheka smiled at his reaction and pulled each other closer to one another. The temperature was perfect outside, and the day was under way.

"Can I play my Gameboy? Pleaseeeeee."

"No but you can put your new shirt on. I want to take of picture of you in it for ever lasting memories." said Sheka while snapping photos of Aayan while posing with his new shirt on.

Walking towards the entrance they stopped to take a family photo in front of the Kings Dominion sign.

"Aayan remember this sign. If you get lost in the park you meet us here as fast as you can." said Sheka.

"Yes maam."

"Now let's go have fun birthday boy." said Keith as he scooped Aayan off his feet.

Ride after ride they enjoyed the day for hours before they went to the waterpark. After setting up in the chairs in front of the wave pool. Keith and Aayan ran to jump in the water while Sheka sat. She stared at them, lowered her head, got up and found the nearest payphone. She looked side to side and over her shoulder before she typed in a beeper number 8045552221 911. The phone rang and she answered on the first ring.

Sheka: It's almost time.

Unknown Person: Rebel Yell 6pm

Sheka hung up the phone and headed back to the chairs. Keith and Aayan was having so much fun they didn't notice that she got up and left. Soon as they were don't in the wave pool, they left to go eat. They let Aayan eat all of the food he wanted for his birthday. He ordered pizza, cheeseburgers, fries and a milkshake. Aayan was full but could not get the Rebel Yell off of his mind. After eating he rubbed his belly, stood up, and ran circles around the table yelling "Rebel Yell".

"Ok, Ok young man calm down. We are going to the rebel yell." said Sheka while looking down at her watch realizing it was 5:50pm.

Hastily moving to the ride, Sheka scanned the area looking for a medical area. Once they got to the line that was long with an approximate 30-minute wait from where they stood, Sheka suddenly dropped to the ground, complained about a sharp pain in her stomach and an inability to see. Keith dropped by her side and began to yell for help as she wallowed in pain.

"Momma are you ok!" said Aayan while looking back forth between her and the roller coaster line.

"She is fine we just have to go find a medic. So come on."

"No Keith let him stay and ride the roller coaster. That's all he has been talking about all this time. The medic station isn't that far, I believe I seen it on the way over here." said Sheka as she continued to wince in pain.

"Ok baby you right. Aayan stay in line. If we aren't back before you are done, sit on this bench and wait for us ok."

"Ok daddy. Get better mommy."

"I will son. Now have fun."

"Rebel Yell, Rebel Yell." said Aayan as he walked forward in the line that shortened because of the scene.

After a long wait Aayan finally made it to the front of the line. Excited about riding the ride of his dreams were crushed by the ride attendant after being told that he was too short to ride. A disappointed Aayan walked down the ramp and sat on the bench where he was instructed to wait. After sitting there for five minutes a stranger came and sat next to him.

"Hey how you doing little man." said the stranger as he reached to shake his hand.

"My parents told me don't talk to strangers." said Aayan as he scooted away.

"I'm not a stranger, I know your parents. You can call me V. You are Aayan correct."

"Yes I'm Aayan. So, you do know my parents. Is my mom ok?"

"She is fine. They told me to come get you. They want you to meet them at the spot you are supposed to meet at if you got lost." said V as he reached for his hand again.

"Ok. I hope my mommy is good." said Aayan as he took V's hand and headed for the gate.

V and Aayan made it to the Kings Dominion sign and sat down. They sat there for two minutes before a red dodge caravan with five percent tent pulled up to the curve. V looked at the driver and gave a head nod. The driver nodded back and reached to slide the side door open. V looked around reached in his pocket and pulled a rag out covering Aayan's nose and mouth. Aayan panicked and began to yell drawing attention from a few people leaving the park.

"MOMMY, DADDY! PLEASE STOP! MOMMY, MOMMY, MOMM, MOM, MO!" yelled Aayan before blacking out.

    V lifted his limp body to the van climbed in, shut the door and slammed Aayan's young limp body on the floor. The driver looked at Aayan in the floor and pulled off laughing as V propped his feet up on Aayan's body. Thirty minutes into the drive Aayan started to regain consciousness and immediately began to scream for Keith and Sheka.

    "Hey monkey shut the fuck up." said V as he lit a cigarette.

    "MOMMA! DA......!" yelled Aayan.

    Before he could finish getting the scream out V punched him in the temple knocking him back out. Before he gained consciousness again V taped his mouth shut, and tied his hands and feet. Aayan was knocked out, but he could subconsciously hear the men talking and laughing in a foreign language. Due to the blunt force trauma Aayan couldn't dream if he wanted to.

    "This black bastard den hurt my damn hand." said V in Russian while laughing out loud.

    Two hours into the drive V decided to play a game with Aayan. He lit cigarettes and put them out on Aayan's skin waking him up and then punching in the face knocking him back out again. V played this game until Aayan's left eye swelled shut and his Simpson shirt was covered with blood. Aayan opened his teary right eye and yelled at the top of his lungs with his mouth gagged. Aayan yelled and cried till he went to sleep. He didn't wake up again till the van stopped. V reached in the back, grabbed a sack filled with dog shit, put it on Aayan's head and tied it closed. That was the last light Aayan seen on his ninth birthday.

"Aayan this is a lot. Are you sure you want to keep going?" said Tamika as she wiped a tear from her eye.

"Yes, I want to keep going. I need to get this out, especially since there are people trying to kill me." said Aayan as he stood staring out the window.

CHAPTER 10
1ST STOP

Waking up with his mouth gagged and his head still covered, Aayan looked thru the little squares in the bag for some type of light. He ran his fingers along the burn marks he had received on the trip to this unknown location and his eyes began to tear. The pain from the knots in his head from the strikes he received from V had begun to return. Panicking he let out loud scream. The scream was nullified by the gag in his mouth.

Feeling around his surrounding he began to realize that he was in a cage, a small cage. The cage had sturdy metal and plastic around it as if it was a dog cage. Filling around more he felt something that felt like a teddy bear in the back of the cage. It didn't move or make a sound. he began to stroke it with his fingertips from his hog-tied hands. The touch of this teddy bear gave him a peace. It made Aayan feel like everything was going to be alright and that he would be home soon. The thoughts were interrupted by the sounds of the news that he could barely hear. Moving his head close as he could to the sound Aayan began to listen.

FOX 5 News Reporter: Good Evening, we are coming to you live from Kings Dominion Amusement Park in Doswell, VA where a nine-year-old boy Aayan King is missing. Sources say he was last seen in the park at the Rebel Yell rollercoaster where he was rejected due to his height. I am standing here with the parents who have been desperately looking for their son for hours.

Reporter: Good Evening Mr. and Mrs. King, I know this is a trying time for you.

"This is supposed to be a safe place for children. How the hell can my son just disappear!" yelled Keith as he held Sheka in his arms tight.

"He is brown skin, 4'8, roughly about 78 pounds. He had on blue shorts and a Simpson's t-shirt that he just received for his birthday." said Sheka.

"Aayan if you are seeing or hearing this, please come to the meeting place. We love you! Please just come to the meeting place." Keith and Sheka said in unison.

"If he is abducted, do you have any words?" said the reporter sticking the mic into Keith's face.

"Bitch our son is missing and you are looking for ratings. How disrespectful of you!" yelled Keith.

"I didn't mean any disre----" being cut off by Sheka.

"If he was abducted and you have him, please bring home. No matter the cost! We want our boy back!"

Hearing the interview made Aayan cry till he passed out. He just wanted to go home and play his Gameboy. Only thing he could dream about was the moment he was lifted and put into the van. The nightmare kept replaying in his mind violently waking him up from being passed out. Closing his eyes again he heard the door open and immediately opened his eyes trying to see who was there. He couldn't make out any of the faces thru the burlap sack and dog feces. He began to listen in hopes of someone being there to help him.

"What the hell are all these burns on him?" said the anonymous man.

"You just said you wanted him. You didn't say in what condition. This was a kidnapping, not a field trip. Now where is the money?" said V as he put his hand on his knife holster.

"Calm down its upstairs in bag on the table."

"OK pay me I have shit to do. I can't be sitting around playing with you and this black bastard all day."

"Shut up man and come on. I need you to come back and get him in a week."

"Whatever you want, as long as you're paying." said V with a smug tone as he jumped up the steps towards the table with the money in the bag.

Sitting in the cage squirming around trying to get free, the sack around Aayan's head began to loosen up. He felt a breath of fresh air from the rope loosening around his neck. Swinging his head back and forth the bag begins to ease its way off. The back-and-forth motion began to make him dizzy, but he wanted to be free. With the bag just about over his nose Aayan began to see a beam of moonlight thru a hole in a darkly taped basement window.

With the corner of his eye, he began to scan the basement for way to escape, but because of how dark it was he could only see shadowy silhouettes of the items in the basement. The site of the items in the basement were terrifying. He turned and began to pet the teddy bear in the back of the cage for relaxation. He continued to try to get the burlap sack off of his head until he heard yelling coming from upstairs. The yelling was violent and loud. It made him freeze in place.

"Motherfucker where is the rest of the money!" yelled V as he beat loudly on the table.

"Half now, half when you come back and pick him up."

"That wasn't the deal you fat piece of shit. Pay me now or I'll take the black bastard with me."

"The boy stays until I am done with him. This is all the money you are getting for now. I need you to leave." said the anonymous man as he opened the basement door, grabbed a bag of Cheetos, a bottled water and began to walk down the stairs.

"Ok that how we are playing it. This isn't done I'll be right back." said V as he scrambled out of the door.

Hearing the footsteps coming Aayan laid back down as if he were sleep. Chills began to take over his body. At the young tender age of nine Aayan was scared of the unknown. He didn't know if he was going to die or if he was going to be abused again. He wanted neither. The steps got closer and Aayan movement became more still out of fear of not know what was going to happen. He started reminiscing about how him and his dad played tag and when he sat perfectly still his dad pretended he couldn't see him as if he were invisible. In his mind he needed that to work now.

"Hey little fella don't be scared ok. I brought you some snacks and water. You are in good hands. Don't you worry. If you can understand me sit up and nod your head." said the anonymous voice.

Aayan sat up and nodded.

"Good. I am going to lift the burlap sack up right above your nose and I am going to ungag you. Please don't scream, I am not here to hurt you. Nod if you understand."

Aayan nodded again. He just wanted to be free, and this seemed like a way out. He heard the door of the cage open and as promised the stranger lifted the sack right above his nose, letting all of the feces out and ungagging his mouth. He took a deep breath and tried to lean the bag back further so he could see, but the restraint wouldn't allow it.

"I am going to untie your hands. Please don't try anything or I will tie you back up and gag your mouth. Do you want that?"

"No." said Aayan.

"Here you go. Eat and drink up. You will be home before you know it."

"I just want my mommy and daddy. Please can I go home." said Aayan as he started to eat the Cheetos and drink the water panting after a big gulp.

"I know you are scared but you are in good hands. You will be home before you know it."

"Can I take this all the way off please. It's scary and I don't like it." said Aayan as he reached back to stroke the teddy bear at the back of the cage.

"No, you can't take it off yet. Be patient." said the anonymous man before there was a loud crash at the front door that startled him and Aayan.

"Where the fuck are you!" yelled V as he scrambled thru the house throwing things around.

Aayan scooted to the back of the cage in fear. He hated the sound of V's voice, it was terrifying. Listening to the chaos, he began to pet the teddy bear in the cage harder and harder for comforter. The footstep and the yelling from V got louder as he made his way down the steep basement steps. The aggression in his voice gave Aayan the chills as he balled up in the corner of the cage.

"Give me all of my money now or give me that black bastard." yelled V while pulling a .357 pistol out of his pants.

"Listen! Calm down I don't have all of the money. I just have what was given to me."

"Give me the boy! No money no boy! Business don't run that way with V.

"V calm down and put the gun down. Let me make a phone call to see if I can get the rest of it today."

"You better or I will shoot you in your legs and feet, kill the boy and burn the house down with you in it alive!" yelled V pointing the gun at Aayan.

"Please don't kill me!" screamed a scared Aayan from the back of the cage.

"You are going to be fine." said the anonymous man.

Acting as if he was walking away the anonymous man lunges at V and a scuffle between them begins over the pistol. Going back and forth they banged into boxes crushing them and fell over old furniture wrapped in plastic. While wrestling for the pistol it fires off two rounds thru the ceiling of the basement scaring Aayan prompting him to close his eyes tight.

"I'm going to kill you motherfucker!" yelled V.

"Run Aayan! Now!" yelled the anonymous man.

Aayan slowly lifted the bag off of his face, looked at the teddy bear he was petting for comfort and screamed at the top of his lungs. The teddy bear was a dead poodle. The poodle was half decayed and had maggots all over it. Aayan looked down at his hands covered in maggot and yelled again. Soon as he looked to exit the cage to run the .357 went off two more times and the wrestling stopped.

Once he got to the door of the cage to exit a man hit the floor in front of the exit blocking it. Moving closer he looked at the battered, still face with his eyes open with blood coming out of his mouth and realized the man was Mr. Witt. A confused Aayan attempted to climb out and run for the stairs, but a tired battered V sat up and grabbed his foot preventing him from getting away.

"Where the hell do you think you are going? You are mine now!" said V as he struck Aayan in the back of the head with the pistol knocking him out.

The violent blow dropped Aayan limp. V grabbed him by his arm and dragged his motionless body bouncing his head off of every step on the way up. Aayan opened his eyes from the pain of his limp body being thrown forcefully into the van. The last thing he heard before he passed out was this.

"That dude is dead. We still need to get the rest of the money. I found the number that he was communicating with when I was tearing the house up. Let's find a payphone and a place to stay the night. If they don't have the money, I know where we can take him and get paid." said V as he slammed the sliding van door shut.

"Randy will pay top dollar for him. Why not just take him there instead of taking the chance of getting caught." said the driver.

"Money... my man... money.... Whoever fat ass was talking to has to have money." said V.

CHAPTER 11
DEMANDS

Sitting in tears Tamika stared at Aayan. She didn't understand how Aayan was so composed telling this story. She closed her notepad and began to tap her foot on the ground watching Aayan stare out of the hospital window. She wondered why he never shared this story with the world. Looking thru her purse she pulled out a circular mirror, opened it and stared at herself. Aayan looked over his shoulder, grabbed a napkin and helped her dab the running make up off of her face.

"We can stop there for the day. I dont think you can handle anymore today." said Aayan walking back to stare out of the window.

"Are you sure? I have a job to do. If you can continue to tell the story, I will continue to listen and take notes." said Tamika as she began to apply make up in the blotched areas.

"I can keep going. Isn't it messed up though? Think about it. It gets worse and deeper. There were demands made. I guess I'll share a little more." said Aayan as he stretched his arms above his head and took a sip of water.

"How do you feel?"

"Normal because this gets worse. I hope you are prepared."

"Continue Aayan that's what I am here for."

Riding in the back of the van for what felt like forever, they finally came to a stop. Laying on the uncomfortable floor in the van Aayan heard the driver ask for $30 on number one. Rolling back in forth in the back of the van, all Aayan could think about was getting home and not dying. The doors on the van opened back up prompting Aayan to stay still. They drove for a little while longer on a bumpy road before they made their final stop.

"You go get the room while I make the call." said V as he looked around easing the sliding door open.

"We are the only ones here; we picked a good motel. Hurry up and make the call." said the driver.

"Cmon bastard get up let's go!" said V while punching Aayan's legs violently.

Walking towards the payphone holding Aayan by the back of his neck firmly V glanced around and whispered to Aayan.

"I am going to take this sack and gag off of you. If you scream or try anything I am going to put a bullet in your temple." said V as he tapped his pistol on Aayan head.

Aayan nodded vigorously in agreement as V lifted the sack off of his head and ungagged his mouth. Looking around trying to familiarize himself with the area Aayan looked at the old brick motel in the middle of nowhere. Only thing that stood out to him was the name of the Motel on the sign wasn't lit up and two letters in the word motel were missing. The sign looked as if the motel had been out of business for years. There was no identifiable address or signs of anyone who could help.

"Time to get this money boy! You want to go home, and I want to get rid of you. When I call, I am going to put you on the phone, so they know you are ok. You better not try anything or else." said V as he pulled Aayan by his bound hands closer to the phone.

"I just want to go home mister please."

Dialing the number that he picked up from Mr. Witts house the phone began to ring. V knew that the call had to be quick so it couldn't be traced. He just wanted to make his demand, let them hear Aayan and give a drop off spot. Easy and straight to the point. V was ready to be rid of Aayan because him being with them wasn't part of the plan. Sitting on the pay phone listening to it ring V smacked Aayan on the back of the head.

"You better hope they answer."

"I just want to go home mister."

After a few more rings V hung and tried it again. His patience wearing thin he began to tap his pistol against his leg The phone ringing was loud enough for Aayan to hear. After a few more rings the phone on the other end was answered.

"Hello, we have your son! We want $200,000 dropped at the blockbuster in Fredrick, Maryland tomorrow at noon." said V as he shoved the phone in Aayan face and gestured for him to speak.

"Breathing on the phone."

"Please I just want to go home! I want my mommy and da........." said Aayan before V snatched the phone back listening to the breathing on the other end.

"Tomorrow noon don't be late."

"You did me a favor killing Witt. You can keep his ass. I don't want him back. I was on the way over here to take care of it myself." said Sheka as she stood at the top of the stairs looking down at Mr. Witts body on the basement floor.

"I'm not playing games I will kill him." said V as he hit Aayan making him scream on the phone.

With the phone to ear before he could plea for help, he heard a raspy but all too familiar voice come thru the phone loud and clear. The voice sent a jolt thru his body as if he were struck by lightning. The pain of what she said made him cry uncontrollably.

"You aren't getting a dime. Fuck him and fuck you. He can suffer before you end him."

"Mommy why?" said Aayan before V snatched the phone and hung up.

"Where are we meeting for the money tomorrow?" said the driver as he walked around the corner with the room key.

"We are going to see Randy. They said fuck this kid!" said V as he gagged and covered Aayan head escorting him into the room where he took him into the bathroom and threw him in the tub.

"See Tamika that was the last time I heard my mother's voice. She wanted me gone. Can you imagine that being a nine-year-old kid?" said Aayan as he looked down at his phone to check the time.

"This is tragic Aayan. My goodness you are a strong man. You have been walking around with all of this bottled up in you." said Tamika as she tapped her pen on the pad in her lap.

"Hold on Tamika. I keep getting text messages let me check them really quick."

"Ok."

Caze: Dude put me on with Tamika. I need that ASAP. I can't believe you been hiding her.

Aayan: I'll see what I can do.

Zack: Are you ok with Caze just signing this paperwork for you?

Aayan: no.

Caze: When are you going to be out of the hospital? We really need to talk! Don't be doing extra therapy in there you creep.

Aayan: I'll be done shortly so we can talk. Did you get the paperwork to Zack?

Zack: Also, on a more serious note. All of the people that are making claims against you said they will go away if you pay them what they request.

Aayan: They are extorting me. I'm not paying them a dime! I told you this already. I'll call when I'm done. Did Caze get the paperwork the paperwork to you?

Caze: Im sending the documents for Zack to review. Put me on with Tamika man.

"Is everything alright?" said Tamika.

"Yeah, I think this fool Caze is in love with you. He wants your number."

"He was cute. I have his card, ill hit him up. Are you ready to continue?"

"Well look at that I am in here playing match maker for rich people. Maybe that should be my job." said Aayan as he hysterically laughed.

"Yeah let's keep going. There isn't much more I want to talk about today. We need to link up tomorrow if you are available after this short piece."

"You have jokes Aayan, now continue."

"I'll check my schedule and have my secretary contact you."

"Now back to my life." said Aayan as he sighed.

Closing his eyes, Aayan could envision the cold bathroom at the Motel and the darkness of having the sack on his head. The chilled porcelain of the tub kept his skinned chilled enough to keep goosebumps on him. The consistent drips from the sink faucet, the constant running toilet and the wind from the cracked window made it impossible to sleep, but the fatigue from the day wouldn't let him stay awake. Aayan's much needed sleep was interrupted by a drunk V who stumbled into the bathroom and began to loudly urinate in the toilet startling him.

"You thirsty you little bastard." said V as he turned and aimed his urine at Aayan.

"Leave the boy alone. Randy aint gonna want him smelling like piss." said the driver standing in the doorway waiting for the bathroom.

"Shut up! Randy will take what we give him. Matter of fact grab the boy lets head there now." said V as he zipped up his pants and turned the shower on as cold as it could get to ensure Aayan was awake.

Grabbing Aayan's wet body out of the tub they headed out to the van. Both men stumbling drunk tripped over the corner of the bed dropping Aayan roughly making him hit his head on the edge of the mini fridge knocking him out cold again. He started coming thru from the brutal hit because of the bumpy ride, the sound of 'Born to be Wild' playing on repeat and the two men tapping on the dashboard and steering wheel. He was awakened all the way when the driver slammed on the brakes forcing his body to slide across the van floor into the van wall.

Pulling into a gated complex the driver slowed down and pressed the buzzer on a screen. The driver smiled with a drunken grin into the camera and in a slurred tone yelled for them to open up. After being buzzed thru the gate they rolled down a long brick driveway. The lawn was neatly trimmed, the bushes cut in the shapes of animals and the lights on the sides of the driveway lit up as the van passed them on the way to the massive mansion at the end of the road.

The house was illuminated as if it was Christmas Day. There was heavily armed security pacing in the yard around the house. They slowly pulled to the front of the mansion where two members of the security was awaiting. The two men were standing with a bag of money. When the van stopped V hopped out and attempted to hug one of the security guards but was pushed away roughly.

"No sense of humor my friend. Where is Randy? Is he too good to handle business himself." said V as he slid the side door open exposing Aayan in the back.

"Why is his head covered like that. Uncover it, you know Randy doesn't like that." said the guard.

"Ok... Ok... Here you go. I present to you... shit I don't know his name but let's call him the black bastard." said V.

"What the hell happened to him? Why were you abusing this child? You know Randy doesn't like that either. Untie him and ungag him now."

"So pushy big man calm down. What he has been thru is no worse than what Randy does." said V as he ungagged and untied Aayan.

Walking out of the house stood a tall, slim, white man with dirty blonde hair dressed in all white. The light shining behind him thru the clear window doors made it look as if he just stepped out of the heavens. The site made Aayan feel as he was about to be saved.

"You don't know what I do. Don't make assumptions or you won't make it off of my property. I haven't fed the hogs in weeks." said Randy while standing at the top of his stone steps just outside of the ten-foot-high door opening.

"Come with me boy." said the second guard as he walked Aayan towards Randy.

"What's your name little one? Did those men hurt you?" said Randy as he squatted and lifted Aayan's head.

"Yes, they hurt me. My name is Aayan. Mister, can I please go to my dad now?"

"Point to the one who hurt you."

Aayan slowly turned around, wiped the tears from his eyes and pointed at V. He put his head down and faced Randy again. Randy turned Aayan to face the van, put his hands on his shoulders and whispered in his ear.

"Keep your eyes open."

"Ok mister." said Aayan as he stared at the bottom of the porch.

"You brought me an injured young man. He did nothing to deserve this treatment. I firmly believe any man that will hurt a child like this doesn't deserve compensation. What do you think Aayan." said Randy as he signaled for the guard to bring the money back.

"Cmon at least half, this is bad business. I didn't mean to hurt the boy. Let me at least pay my driver he had nothing to do with it." said V as he stood with his arms open.

"You want half. Ok I will give you half… half of everything." said Randy as he nodded at the guard.

The guard turned around raised his weapon and shot V in his arms, legs, feet and stomach. He then walked to the van dropped the money in the passenger seat and told the driver to leave or he would meet the same fate. The driver began to tear up as he looked at V on the ground yelling for help.

"Please don't kill him! You can have the money back we will leave and never comeback. Please!" screamed the driver.

"Take the money and leave now." said the guard as he raised the gun towards the driver.

He slowly pulled off looking in the rearview mirror beating on the steering wheel crying. Reaching in the bag of money in the passenger seat to see the amount, the driver wiped his tears and stared at the long driveway trying to focus before he heard a voice come from the house. He pulled over outside the gate and watched thru binoculars.

"Feed him to the hogs alive and put his teeth in the jar." said Randy as he walked away with his arm around Aayan.

Aayan was fascinated by the look of the house when he walked in. There were statues, paintings and modern furniture all over the house. He was in awe but all he could think about was the last thing he heard his mother say on the phone. He just wanted to know why. At this point he was unsure if he wanted to go home after hearing her. He just hoped that his father didn't feel the same way.

"See Tamika hearing how Randy handled V you would have thought his home was a safe haven. It wasn't but we can discuss that in the next session. Is that cool with you."

"Yes, I think that's a good stopping point for the day. How are you feeling."

"Good, I feel like I'm starting to get the weight off my shoulders."

"Ok let's do a breathing exercise to diffuse this session. I know you have a lot of important business to take care of."

"Let's do it... you just make sure you hit Caze up, so he leaves me alone about you."

"I will."

Leaving the hospital with his heavily armed security, Aayan got to his vehicle and noticed that Avery wasn't driving today. All he could do was hope that he wasn't injured in anyway or was forced to quit by the henchman trying to kidnap him. Stepping into the vehicle he immediately scanned the vehicle for anything wrong.

"Where is Avery?" said Aayan in a state of confusion.

"He couldn't be here today sir. He called in." said the driver.

"Are you sure he wasn't kidnapped or is in danger?"

"He has a security detail watching him. He is fine."

Still confused why Avery wasn't driving him, Aayan called his phone and it went straight to voicemail. He called Caze and his phone went to voicemail as well. He then called Herb. Noone answered the phone. His level of concern had risen to an intolerable level as he continued to make calls around. He called Bryan and Byron there was no answer. He then received a call from Zack, but this call was a pocket dial and was muffled. Aayan yelled for Zack to pick up, but he could tell the phone was in his pocket or laptop case.

Staying on the phone listening he heard three voices, but he couldn't make them out. He did know one of them was Zack for sure. He didn't know if he was having a meeting with the people trying to extort him or was this just a regular meeting for him before he heard one voice loud and clear that sounded like Caze.

"Aye fuck him, are we doing this or not! I am tired of the talking and waiting around. You two clowns keep playing there are things that have to be done!" yelled Caze thru the muffled call.

Aayan knew this had to have something to do with business. Caze was very passionate about his work. Then he heard a muffled Zack and an indiscreet voice begin to talk as if they were trying to calm Caze.

"Calm down man. Why you so amped up." said Zack.

"Agreed mellow out young man... things are going the way they are supposed to right now. Just stay the course." said the third voice.

"Well man hurry up! I'm tired of this shit!" yelled Caze as he walked out.

Zack reached in his pocket and seen the phone was on and quickly hung up. Aayan in a state of confusion didn't have the energy at the moment to try to figure it out. He just wanted to go home, relax, check emails and listen to music. He did send a text to Tamika and Caze during the ride.

Aayan: Tamika, please make sure you use Caze number.

Tamika: I just talked to him. We are going out for a drink tonight.

Aayan: Ok cool. I don't want him getting on my nerves.

Aayan: Caze you lucky dog... you better hit it for me.

Caze: Shut up man, but good looking out

Aayan: I don't want to get to much into it, but I heard you going off earlier. Zack phone pocket dialed me. Are you ok?

Caze: Yeah I'm good. You know how I get when it comes to business.

Aayan: Was it about the paperwork?

Caze: Amongst other things, but that was the focal point.

Aayan: Be patient like that third person said and enjoy your date tonight.

Looking thru his phone, Aayan started playing candy crush on the ride home. His side was still sore from the stitches, but he attempted to block out the pain. Closing his eyes on the ride home Aayan began trying to figure out who and what the next move was. He didn't know when he was going be attacked again and what the meeting was about. Then he giggled thinking about the thought of Caze and Tamika going on a date.

CHAPTER 12
LOOKS ARE DECEIVING

Later that day Caze and Tamika met up at a cozy tavern in Harlem. With the busy schedules they both had they agreed to meet up for a small meal and a drink. The restaurant was crowded despite the restrictions the mayor had just put on the city. Sitting in the chair waiting for Tamika to show up Caze started staring at the TV that was playing CNN. In disbelief he shook his head as the news anchor began his broadcast with a breaking story about the governor of New York resigning due to sexual assault allegations. Checking his phone for the time he was tapped on the shoulder.

"Did I have you waiting too long?" said Tamika as Caze stood to pull her chair out.

"I would have sat here for a week waiting on you."

"Is that so?"

"Damn right." said Caze as he shifted his attention back to the TV to see the next story titled (Monster with Money, who is Aayan Petworth?)

"Are you ok? What's wrong?" said Tamika demanding Caze's attention back.

"Nothing I need to know what's going on with this fool. If they can get the governor, they can get him."

"What fool are you referring to? I am assume Aayan."

"Yeah him... he has so much going on that we just don't understand. He is a real secretive person for no reason. I just want to know if these allegations are true or false, and why people are trying to kill him. I'm sure he is sharing with you, can you give me any inside info. Has he discussed any of it with you?" said Caze in a concerned tone.

"You know I can't discuss that. It's confidential. Maybe you should sit down and talk with him and express your concerns. Is this why you wanted this date? To discuss your boss."

"I'm sorry. How was your day? I didn't mean to start off like this. Especially for a woman who may be my future ex-wife." said Caze as he began to laugh and reach for Tamika's hand.

"Is that so?"

"I mean as long you aren't crazy from dealing with crazy people all day." said Caze as he began to laud hysterically.

"Ok mister funny man. So, what do you do with your life besides slave for Aayan and lie to pretty women." said Tamika as she let out a laugh.

"And you say I have jokes. I am just your run of the mill single guy. I like traveling, working out, movies, bowling, sex, especially the sex...."

"You had to throw sex in there. That made me lose my appetite." said Tamika as she looked away.

"My baa…" said Caze before he was cut off by Tamika.

"For food." said Tamika as she turned and stared in Caze's eyes.

"Oh, is that right?" said Caze as he closed the tab.

"I mean we can stay here and eat, or we can leave, and I can feed you."

Grabbing her by the hand they made their way towards the door. Standing at the valet he put his arm around her and began to run his hands up and down her back. She looked up at the sky and began rubbing Caze's chest. Inching in front of him pushing her body firmly on his, she grabbed Caze's crouch area softly and whispered in his ear.

"You better know what to do with this."

"That's my car right there... you about to find out."

After a long passionate night of love making. Caze woke up from the constant vibrating of Tamika's phone coming from her purse. He stood up to silence the phone, but out of curiosity he looked at some of the messages that came across the locked screen. Looking over his shoulder to ensure she was still asleep, he started reading.

> Aayan: Hey tomorrow can we do therapy early I will need a few hours.
>
> Madam B: Hey things are moving along as planned. Keep up the good work. I will reach out to you once we have him.
>
> Old Ass: Be sure to let me know when he done.
>
> Jerry: I hate you. You freak bitch you gonna smash once and never talk to me again. I hope you die.
>
> YVB: I want my money you better not forget it. There is no guarantee how the product will arrive.

Caze looked over his shoulder again and began to think to himself "what the hell is going on?". He was starting to think Tamika was a part time drug dealer. Looking out the window and then back down at the phone he was interrupted by Tamika's seductive voice.

"What are you doing over there? Come get back in the bed, I need this thirst quenched. You told me I was about to find out... I need you to finish showing me." said Tamika as she laid her naked body on her back playing with herself and waving Caze over with a finger.

"Your phone was going off I was just silencing it." said Caze as he licked his lips looking at her playing with herself.

"Come silence me."

An hour later they laid in the bed sweaty holding each other as the sun began to come up. Kissing her on the forehead, he started thinking about the text in her phone. He began to wonder what she really had going on in her life. In deep thought he was interrupted by Tamika's phone vibrating again.

"You should probably get that. Oh, and when I silenced your phone and Aayan said he needed you early today." said Caze as he released Tamika so she could get up to get the phone.

"Thank you for that. I'll call him right after I get home." said Tamika as she picked up her phone to read the messages.

Tamika's whole demeanor changed reading the messages. She looked down at the messages in her phone, looked over at Caze and scrambled to get dressed. She seemed distraught about something she read and Caze noticed it.

"Are you ok? What's wrong?"

"Yeah, I am fine. I just have to go. I have to get ready for Aayan's session today."

"Oh, I thought you were upset about the angry boyfriend text you got." said Caze as he hopped up to get dressed.

"Angry boyfriend text? Did you go thru my phone?"

"No... I just silenced your phone and there were a few on the locked screen."

"Ohh that wasn't nothing. Just a dumb one-night stand that he can't let go."

"I understand why. That thang is good as hell. When is the next time we gonna link up?"

"I'll let you know. Hit me or ill hit you up, but I have to go my Uber is almost here."

"Uber? I could have taken you to get your car."

"No, I am good. I have some stops to make before I get back to my car. Thanks for the good night. We have to do it again." said Tamika as she walked towards the door in a hurry.

"Ok don't be out here dropping the juice off then letting me die of thirst. That's why that guy was crazy." said Caze as he began to laugh, he heard the door shut.

Looking out the window he watched her hop in and Uber. She looked up waving as if she knew he would be looking out the window. He smiled and walked away beating on his chest and talking to himself. "Good shit my boy" he said repeatedly before picking up his phone to brag about it.

Caze: Boy you therapist aint gonna have no energy today.

Aayan: What you talking about?

Caze: I got the drawls man. It was some fire too. She a freak. I think I'm going to keep her.

Aayan: You nasty mofo. It looks like it's good, but what appointment are you talking about. I don't have one with her till tomorrow.

Caze: You didn't text her last night and say you needed to see her early because you needed a few hours.

Aayan: Nawl man it wasn't me. You sure you saw my name.

Caze: Positive man and it aint many people out here with your name.

Aayan: Maybe you were drained from the coochie and was thinking about me, To remind yourself to tell me.

Caze: I know what I saw fool. It was good but it wasn't that good.

Aayan: It may have been an old message.

Caze: Maybe, I would call to make sure there wasn't a scheduling mix up.

Aayan: I call her later and clear it up. Now get your ass up and go to work.

Caze: I'm working from home today. I have to go see Zack later.

Aayan: Ok... later man.

Caze: Later and be safe Batman. I know you relaxing and recovering.

Aayan sat at the foot of his bed, double checked his calendar and scratched his head. There was no therapy appointment scheduled for today. To clear up the confusion he called Tamika.

"Good morning, Tamika, I don't have an appointment scheduled with you today do I?"

"No, it was an old message. I take it you talked to your friend."

"I did... Yall nasty." said Aayan as he began to laugh.

"We grown out here. I have to go just come ready to talk tomorrow. You need to rest anyway."

"I will have a good day see you tomorrow."

CHAPTER 13
RANDY

The day of rest Aayan took was well needed. He was still sore from yet another attempt on his life. The mystery behind it was mind bending. He knew he had a past but that was long gone and over with. Aayan had grown to be a very structured person. The chaos and confusion had taken him out of his focus. He was just happy to keep it under control in front of people.

Taking a deep breath in, he stared out the window admiring the city. It was his favorite thing to do. Rubbing the wound on his side, Aayan decided that he wanted to do therapy from the comfort of his home. The environment wasn't stressful, he didn't have to venture out into the unknown and he was paying Tamika enough to make house calls.

After taking a hot shower to get his mind right, he called Tamika and changed the location of therapy. He knew it was going to be a long session. It was time to really start digging deep and getting things off of his chest. The next few sessions would be the hardest for him. Not only would it be mentally and emotionally draining, but the sessions would be physically draining as well from all of the pacing back and forth he knew he would be doing.

Three hours later Aayan received a call from his security informing him that Tamika had arrived. Reviewing his camera by the elevator to ensure it was her, he gave them the go ahead to let her up. Staring at the screen he watched Tamika look around as if she was either amused or lost. Security escorted her to the elevator where she took what felt like a long ride up to Aayan. When the door opened, she was greeted by his smiling face.

Stepping off of the elevator Tamika began to look around as if she was trying to assess Aayan living conditions. She was good at her job so tying client's trauma to the way they lived was an area of expertise. Staring at the paintings on the walls and peeping into the kitchen area she could tell his home was a complete bachelor pad.

"Good morning, Tamika, are you ready for today? I have a lot to talk about." said Aayan breaking her away from looking around.

"You really live a humble life I see. I was expecting more from a billionaire."

"Life is simple. It's the people you invite in it that make things complicated."

"Is that why you isolate yourself to a point that you only have one way in or out. Unless you have a secret stairway outside of that window."

"I like to control who I deal with, and you will learn a major reason why today. Since you are analyzing me does that me the session has started."

"It starts when you're ready. I am just looking around."

"Let's have a seat. I am ready." said Aayan pulling out two cushioned chairs at his table.

"Ok, we left off with... what did you say his name was... Randy." said Tamika pulling out her pen and pad.

"Yes... Randy." said Aayan as he began to tap the table repeatedly.

"Take a deep breathe, get your nerves together."

"Ok…Fast forward two years, I was a 11-year-old boy and the search for me was over. The thought of me going home was gone. Randy's house was my home. The thought of the things he made me do sickens me. I was on drugs heavily, heroin to be exact. I was fighting for fun sometimes killing kids for the amusement of him and his friends. The different sexual acts I had to perform is the reason I believe I am single now. Tamika the man was a monster. I stayed because I didn't know how to leave or where I would go. Once I got to the house I never left, Randy wouldn't let me."

"Sounds horrific."

"It was... I thought he was a good guy. He was a monster. I still hear his voice calling for me."

Flashing back to Randy's house, Aayan began to sweat and rub his arms. The voice is one that he would never forget. He heard his tone in every inflection that was ever spoken to him. Especially in the last days of being in the house.

"Aayan hurry and finish eating, there is somebody I want you to meet." said Randy as he sat the basement.

Hurrying thru his cerea,l he ran to the basement in a hurry to see Randy sitting in his throne. A throne he seen him sit in too many times when something was about to happen for amusement. Aayan's mood immediately changed. He hated that chair and everything it stood for.

"Aayan, my little champion. Come to me." said Randy waving him over.

"Yes Mr. Randy." said Aayan as he stood next to the throne.

"You see those men. They want to hurt me. They want to hurt you. They want to take your fun medicine away and make you homeless again. Do you want that?"

"No."

"That boy that is with them, I want you to beat him to death, cut him up and feed him to the pigs. Before you feed him to the pigs, I will give you your happy medicine."

"Do I have to? Can we just go outside and play instead." said Aayan as he looked over at the scared little boy hiding behind one of the men.

"You will do as your told or I will feed you to the pigs alive. Do you understand me boy?" said Randy smacking Aayan in the back of the head knocking him into the middle of the blood-stained floor.

The little boy couldn't have been older than nine. He looked the same age as Aayan when he was abducted. The boy began to scream as the men forced him to the middle of the floor to stand opposite of Aayan. A lot of young children held in captivity heard horror stories of the things that happen in the basement with the red floor. Abducted children feared the basement more than the horrors of captivity itself.

"Please don't! I don't want too!" yelled the boy.

Aayan looked over his shoulder at Randy who was signaling to attack the boy. He looked back at the boy who was trying to flee and rushed at him, striking him in the side of the face knocking him off balance. The disoriented boy turned around with tears in his eyes and was struck again as the men began to cheer the fight on. He struck the boy again in his stomach forcing him to fold over. Aayan whispered in his ear.

"Swing back or they will kill us both. The third time you hit me, I am going to grab your arm and we are gonna run for the stairs."

The boy looked up and struck Aayan in the face with all his might knocking him to the ground. The yelling from the men became deafening in the basement. The sun light shining from the basement door became motivation for the boy as he struck Aayan's face again making him see stars. He was struck a third time thinking that was the sign to go but the boy looked in Aayan's eyes and saw the blows he dealt did real damage. The thought of escaping transformed to the thought of actually winning the fight. This brought on a sense of urgency over the boy as he began to throw blow after blow. A dazed Aayan filtering thru all of the noise could only hear one voice... Randy's.

"Fight back you black bastard. Fight back or I will feed you to the pigs."

Shaking off the blows he had received Aayan looked at the boy moving forward and mouthed the words "Let's Go" turning his head towards the basement door. He let the boy swing three more times dodging all three. To convince the men the fight was going to continue Aayan rear back and swung as hard as he could and turned to run for the door expecting to be followed before he heard a thud. He turned around to see the lifeless boy laying on the floor. The punch connected directly to his temple killing him instantly.

Aayan looked at the boy and bolted for the door as fast as he could. The last words he heard before he ran was Randy's voice.

"Come feed him to the pigs NOW!"

All he could think was not another kid as he sped out the back of the house into the woods that led into the mountains. Aayan was done with the fighting, the drugs and Randy. Without a plan, food or money he kept running till his body told him that he needed to take a break. Finding a waterfall area, he kneeled down and grabbed water with both hand drinking to quench his thirst. Looking around taking in the beautiful sites of nature, he looked down at his reflection in the water, got up and continued to run till the sun went down.

Nestling up in a cave right under an overhang, Aayan found a soft patch of grass in the rock filled area. Laying down he began to listen to the sounds of the owls hooting, the grasshoppers chirping and the wind blowing. It was comforting. The kind of comfort he hadn't felt in a while. The peace Aayan felt was enough for him to fall asleep for a few hours before he was awakened by two strangers with hunting rifles.

"Hey buddy what you doing way out here?" said the first stranger as he took a step closer.

"What's your name little man? Where are your parents?" said the second stranger.

"Can you talk buddy? Its ok you are safe now." said the first stranger as he laid his rifle down and reached his hand out.

"I'm Aayan and I just want to go home."

"Where is home buddy? We can get you there."

"I am from Brandywine, Md." said Aayan as he stood and moved into the moonlight.

"Holy shit. It's that boy from the news that went missing a few years ago." said the second stranger as he reached for a candy bar in his pocket.

"Is that who you are?" said the first stranger.

"Yes, it's me."

"We need to get you home. I'm sure your parents are worried sick about you. Let's go." said the second stranger as he handed Aayan the candy bar.

Quickly unwrapping the candy bar Aayan followed the men out to the main trail. The men talked about different things along the way, mostly about how they were going to be labeled heroes for finding him. After a short walk Aayan began to see lights over the ledge and that excited him extremely. Up the slight incline sat a tinted-out Astro Van. Aayan got a chill of fear. The last time he seen a van he was kidnapped and that was unsettling, forcing him to take steps backwards.

"It's ok buddy. We gonna get you home. Cmon over here."

"Are we really gonna go to my home? I don't want to go anywhere else." said Aayan in a mumbling tone.

"Hop in." said the second stranger.

Stepping into the open door, Aayan immediately let out a scream of terror as he tried to rush back out the door before it shut and locked. He tried beating on the window, but they would not break. He closed his eyes and slumped into the seat.

"Was all of that necessary. After all I have done for you." said Randy sitting in the back seat with the severed head of the boy from the fight positioned next to him.

"Mr. Randy."

"Ahhh, aahhh, ahhh. You ungrateful black bastard. I fed you, clothed you... I insured you had everything that you needed, and you ran away from me. You fucking ran away from me!" yelled Randy as he threw the severed head at Aayan.

"Tamika I was tortured for two weeks before I was trafficked overseas. They tied me by hands so my feet could barely touch the ground in the hog pen just out of their reach. He didn't feed the hogs for weeks at a time. They did all they could to try to get to me. Between that, the daily lashes, and being pumped with heroin I really didn't care about life anymore. They fed me enough to keep me alive. I just wanted to die, but he wouldn't let me " said Aayan as he took a sip of water. said Aayan leaning back in his chair.

"My goodness Aayan."

"There was one security guard that would try to sneak me food. They were only feeding me enough to barely keep me alive. He was the one who told me I was being sent to Germany with the next shipment. He told me that kids never come back once they get over there. Imagine hearing that as a child."

"How do you feel about Randy?"

"He got what he deserved. That's all I am going to say about that. Men like him deserve what they get." said Aayan while looking at his watch.

"Do you have somewhere to be?"

"No, just looking we have a lot of time left."

"Do you want to continue with Randy and how he got what he deserved?"

"No, I want to move forward about what happened when I arrived in Germany."

"Ok."

"This is horrible. You are strong. How do you feel about it now?"

"I don't feel. That's why I hired you. I know how I felt about him at the moment. I wanted to kill him, especially after I found out I was being sold to a buyer in Germany."

"So, you felt anger, frustration and animosity."

"Everything... I felt all of that. I wanted him dead, and I knew I would figure out a way to do it."

"Did you go thru with killing him?"

"He got what he deserved and that's all I will say about that."

Tamika stared at Aayan, opened a bottle of water and suggested they continue.

CHAPTER 14
BUCK BREAKING

"It felt like forever since I had seen sunlight. We were being smuggled overseas in containers with holes in them on oil rigs. The movement of the waves made some of the kids in the container sick. The smell of vomit and unbathed kids was nauseating. After four days in the container, I begun to understand why I was told kids never made it back. Kids were starting to die of thirst and starvation. At nighttime men would come in the container and remove the kids who had passed and gave water and food to the survivors. They did it every three days as if it was survival of the fittest. Once I got to Germany I understood completely. There was no warmup to the life. You were sold to the highest bidder at private auctions and was put straight to work." said Aayan as he got comfortable in his seat.

"That sounds horrible. Do you blame Randy for this?" said Tamika as she looked up from her notepad.

"Why are you bringing up Randy? Of course. This was his fault, he could have sent me home. Instead, he sent me to hell."

"Is this why you say he got what he deserved. I am asking about him because he is a source of pain."

"We can get back to him later. He isn't that important right now." said Aayan in an annoyed tone.

"He is important Aayan. That's why I am asking about him. You say this man got what he deserved. What does that mean to you? What happened between you and him that makes you feel like he got what he deserved." said Tamika as she began to take notes.

"Can we save Randy for later. Can I please tell you what happened once I got to Germany?"

"Ok, but we are going to get back to this Randy thing."

"I was in Germany for two hours before I was bought for a lousy $1300 dollars and a couple of lines of cocaine. Do you know how that made me feel?" said Aayan.

"I can't imagine."

Shortly after being purchased, Aayan was put in a yellow Volvo four-door where he sat quietly in the back as he was told to. Being in a foreign country not knowing what to expect at such a young age he knew compliance was a must. Sitting in the back with three other kids who were purchased two girls and a boy, he sat silently and stared at them. They all looked equally as terrified on the short ride to what looked like an abandoned building. Shortly after parking, the passenger got out, opened the door and began to shout instructions.

"Get your asses out of the car now!" yelled the man in a German tone grabbing one of the screaming girls.

"Sir, where are we going?" said the little boy.

"Shut up filth and stand by the stairs." said the man as he pushed the four kids up the stairs into the building.

Walking down the hallway the horrified kids began to tear up from the yelling and screaming coming from behind the closed doors on the long dark hallway. There were voices of people screaming for help, yelling to be released and begging for food and water. This building was no typical old place. It was a holding point where kids were brought to be broken in. They used it as an in processing to the new life that all the abductees and kidnap victims were going to lead.

Approaching the last room, the man opened it and pushed the kids in. The room had four mattresses on the floor, a toilet, a bucket, a TV that was connected to a VCR and a VHS that said play me and never turn me off. The scared kids huddled together on one mattress as the man walked to the TV and VCR turned it on and put the VHS in. Turning the volume up as loud as it goes the man waved for the kids to come sit down. They slowly went, sat down, and began to watch the TV.

"This TV is to never be turned off under any condition. Do you kids understand me." said the man.

All of the kids nodded and began to watch the screen as the man left the room locking the door behind him. On the screen was an older white man in a clown suit. He sat down in a skull shaped chair and began to speak very loudly forcing the kids to cover their ears.

"HELLO BOYS AND GULLS. " yelled the clown as he began to honk his loud horn and adjust his volume.

"It's so loud." said Aayan as he stared at the bricked-up windows behind the TV.

"That was just a mic check kiddos. Now that I have your attention…YOU BELONG TO ME NOW. You will do what you are told while you belong to me. You will eat when I tell you to eat, you will sleep when I tell you to sleep, you will shit, shower and pee when I tell you and you will leave here and do what you are told when I tell you in this video. Next don't ever turn this video off or this will happen to you. Don't look away or you are next." said the clown as he laughed at a gagged man tied to a chair being dragged into the room.

The terrified kids stared at the man in the chair as the clown stood up, poured gas on the man and set him on fire. The girls tried to cover their eyes, but Aayan looked at them shook his head no and pulled their hands down. The man screams thru the gag were treacherous, but the kids watched till the man stopped moving in the chair. The clown danced around the fire and continued to chant.

"You belong to me, don't be like him. You belong to me, don't be like him." repeated the clown over and over again before he stopped, stared at the camera thoroughly, and yelled "NOW SLEEP!".

The kids scrambled to the same bed and laid down closing their eyes tightly forcing themselves to sleep. After two hours of lying there Aayan opened his eyes to see the other little boy staring at him. Aayan looked over at the static on the TV and looked back at the boy.

"What's your name?" whispered Aayan inching closer to the boy.

"My name is Julius and yours?"

"I am Aayan."

"That's a different name. Did they take you from Africa or something." said Julius as he made a monkey face laughing.

"Did they take you from the NBA with that old fart name." said Aayan making the face of an old man with no teeth.

"We have to protect each other while we are here. We are like a family now. We have to move as a group. How old are you?"

"I don't know what day it is, but I think I am about to turn 12 if I haven't already."

"Cool I'm 11. How old were you when you got taken?"

"I was 9 and you?"

"9 for me too. See we the kidnapped kinfolk."

"Kinfolk?" said Aayan with a puzzled look on his face.

"Yeah, down south we call relatives, family and friends… kinfolk."

"We should try to go back to sleep. We don't know what time we have to get up kinfolk." said Julius rolling over and closing his eyes, Aayan did the same.

After a few short hours of sleep a loud voice came from the TV. "WAKE UP!" It was the clown ready to start the buck breaking process. Julius and Aayan sprung up looking around and noticed the two girls were gone. They looked at each other and moved quickly to the front of the TV where the clown was sitting in his skull thrown repeating his chant.

"You belong to me, don't be like him. You belong to me, don't be like him. Now repeat after me boys. We belong to you; we will do what we are told."

They sat in front of the TV for the rest of that day staring and chanting. They were so into the chant they didn't notice food was brought into the room. Eight hours into the chanting the screen went blank. The clown reappeared with his eyes in the camera startling the boys.

"EAT!" yelled the clown.

The boys turned around looked and seen to trays sitting on the floor with 2 cheeseburgers, french fries, milk, water and a snickers bar. The boys hastily ate everything except the tray. They sat there, stared at each other and began to say the chant to each other over and over again until the TV cut back on giving them instructions.

"SLEEP!" yelled the clown.

The two ran to the bed and laid down. Out of fear of being taken in the middle of the night they held each other tightly. After a month of this cycle the brotherly bond grew between them. The repetition put their bodies on a natural clock. After the third week they were sitting in front of the TV before it came on and was already saying the chant. On the fourth week they got up to beat the TV and chant but, the clown came on, said nothing, pointed and waved.

The boys looked behind them and on the ground was a 12 pack of Heineken and a mound of cocaine. The two looked at each other and the clown spoke.

"Follow my instructions in this order... Do one line of cocaine, take a sip of beer and fill the baggies in the middle. Do that once and then I want you to drink beer and fill the baggies till the mound is gone. Do you understand?"

"Yes." said the boys in unison as they went over and followed the instructions.

After the line both boys became disoriented and couldn't open the cans of beer. They began to giggle and roll on the floor completely forgetting the task at hand. The irritated clown stared at the screen turning his face side to side and ended the fun quickly.

"YOU FAILED YOUR TASK! FIGHT EACH OTHER NOW!"

The clowns voice quickly sobered the boys up as they stood up faced each other and began to violently fight until they were both bloody, bruised and tired. Wrestling on the floor until they were told to stop the two boys looked at each other and tried not to smile. Aayan pulled Julius close as if he was choking him. He punched Julius in the ribs and began to whisper.

"Brothers fight you wimp."

"STOP! SLEEP!" yelled the clown prompting the boys to run to their respective beds.

The hours of sleep they were allowed felt like minutes to the bruised and battered boys. Coming down from the high had the boys feeling like they had fought grown men. They looked over and smiled at each other pointing across at each other's bruises and cuts. They had grown accustomed to the harsh environments that they had endured thru out the years, so to them this was just another stop on their journey, well so they thought. The boys got up and stood in front of the TV as usual waiting for the clown to appear. They nudged each other with elbows playfully awaiting before the clown appeared staring silently at the boys.

"Eat." said the clown making the boys look over their shoulders at food that was placed in the room while they were staring at the clown.

They walked over sat down and quickly consumed the bacon cheeseburgers, fries, yogurt and juice. The clown watched them eat the food. He began to smile and laugh. Attempting to stand to get back in front of the TV Aayan felt disoriented. He began to hallucinate making him stumble against the door where he was pushed by a man who dropped a knife on the floor. The hallucination made the butchers knife look like He Mans swords. Aayan picked it up screaming.

"I HAVE THE POWER!" yelled Aayan holding the butcher's knife in the air.

Aayan's hallucinations made Julius look like Skeletor. He swung the knife at him. With a confused look on his face, Julius jumped back away from the knife swing and put his back against the wall firmly.

"Aayan what are you doing. Stop! We are the kidnapped kinfolk!" said Julius as he dodged another knife swing.

"Shut up Skeletor! It's time to die." said Aayan swinging the knife again this time striking Julius in his side.

"Stop it please! They did something to you! You are my brother! Please remember!" screamed Julius as his arm was cut by a stark mad Aayan.

Julius began to run around the room bleeding looking for something to defend himself with no success. The pleas from him went unheard by a hallucinating Aayan. Julius fled to his left before he was stabbed in the leg by Aayan who screamed in joy for striking what he thought was Skeletor. Falling to the ground in agony Julius screamed excessively.

"Aayan no! PLEASE!" yelled Julius as Aayan pulled the knife from his leg making blood shoot in the air onto his face.

"AHHHHH! STOP!" yelled Julius!

"DIE SKELTOR DIE!" yelled Aayan as he repeatedly stabbed Julius until he bled out and stopped moving.

"YAY I WON! BY THE POWER OF GREYSKULL!" yelled Aayan pulling the knife out of Julius chest raising it in the air while licking the blood off of his other hand.

Running around the room until he crashed and fell asleep Aayan woke up a few hours later covered in blood looking for a soothing smile from Julius. Instead, there was Julius bloody castrated body. He looked on his blood-filled mattress and saw a knife and severed genitalia. He began to have a panic attack, the excessive sweating, pounding of his heart and shaking of his hands made him pass out again. Waking up again he looked for Julius but this time he was gone, and the bloody floor had been cleaned as much as possible.

"Where is Julius?" yelled Aayan beating on the TV.

The clowned appeared and started to chant turning the switch on within Aayan. Aayan never found out what happen to Julius or his body.

"Tamika, I think we should stop there for the day."

"Did you ever find out what happened to the boy?"

"No, I never found out. I never went to look. I was being broken for months. Everything I was enduring made me forget about him."

"What made you remember him now."

"I feel pain, he was my friend. I just wish his parent could have at least got his body back."

"How do you know they didn't?" said Tamika as she began to gather her things.

"I don't!" said Aayan standing to escort Tamika to the elevator.

"Next session we are going to tap back into this Randy thing before we go any further."

"What's your obsession with him?" said Aayan.

"Just trying to get to the root of things." said Tamika as the elevator closed.

CHAPTER 15

HELL ON EARTH

After an intense therapy session Aayan sat in silence to gather his thoughts about everything he just talked about. He began to think about Julius, the clown, and how long he was actually there being manipulated. There was so much that went on during that year and a half that he would never forget. Aayan then began to wonder if Tamika would break the confidentiality clause to report the murders he had confessed to. He knew there weren't any statutes of limitations on murder. With everything going on in life Aayan knew he couldn't afford for valuable information like that to be leaked to the public. Taking a deep breath and closing his eyes Aayan tried to clear his mind but was startled by a phone call he was receiving from Caze.

"Wassup Caze."

"Wassup Batman. Did you go on any adventures that I need to know about." said Caze while hysterically laughing.

"Shut up man. I just got done with therapy."

"OK right in time remember you have a press conference today. You can't miss this man so get your sad, lonely, boring ass up."

"I forgot about that man. What time and where?"

"It's at 3pm on the steps of the Petworth Promise Foundation headquarters. Be there at 2pm so we can go over your speech and responses for questions that you may receive. Especially if you just randomly come out and say you are a superhero at night."

"Shut up man. I'll be there."

Later that afternoon Aayan made it to his vehicle with a heavily armed security detail. Walking out the door he looked up admiring the beautiful sun filled day. The aroma that filled the air didn't quite meet the match of the look. It smelled like trash and pollution, but still made the day peaceful. Just a regular NYC day. Looking in the vehicle as the door opened, Aayan smiled widely at the site of Avery behind the wheel.

"Mr. Aayan sir, it so good to see you. How do you feel?" said Avery as they began to pull off to the press conference.

"I feel like a circulated dollar Avery. I feel like I have been everywhere and nowhere at the same time." said Aayan gently sliding to the middle seat.

"I can imagine with the hospital stay and all the stuff in the news."

"Yep."

"Are you prepared for today?"

"As ready as I'm going to be. I cant run from everything going on forever."

"You sure cant young man. You sure cant." said Avery as he followed the convoy of trucks heading to the press conference.

Arriving at the press conference there was a sea of people waiting. There were news reporters, journalist, police officers, protesters and supporters. The most notable of all of the people in the crowd were the protesters holding signs in the air. The signs read all sorts of things such as "VACCINES ARE THE EVIL AND YOU ARE THE DEVIL", "RAPIST SHOULD BE SODMIZED ON PUBLIC TV", "MONEY DOESN'T MEAN YOU SHOULD POISON YOUR PEOPLE", "ILLUMINATI OWNS YOUR SOUL", and my favorite "FUCK THE VACCINE. Examining the podium area Aayan exited the vehicle in a hail of flashing camera lights and people yelling. He looked back at Avery as he yelled.

"The truth shall set you free. There are people in the world that want to understand you."

Aayan made it to the podium where Caze was standing with security to his left and right. He looked at the crowd, took a deep breath, looked over his shoulder at Caze and gave him a thumbs up. He looked up at the sun glaring thru the skyscrapers, smiled and open his speech book. The noise of the crowd silenced as Aayan began to speak.

"Good evening guests, media, ladies and gentlemen. I would like to thank all of you for your attendance today." Before he could get any further into his speech there were two loud cracks in the air that sounded like sonic booms prompting everyone to duck. Shortly after hearing the sound, two security guards next to Aayan dropped to the ground bleeding out from shots to the head.

"SNIPER!" yelled a member of Aayan's security detail as he grabbed him by the collar and pulled him in between the team of remaining security guards. Shots began to ring out all over the podium area hitting everyone except for Caze and the security detail escorting Aayan back to his vehicle. All of the police officers began to seek cover to return fire to the area where they assumed the shots were coming from. Aayan watched as a squad of police officers made their way into the building across the street in attempt to catch the shooters.

Hopping in the vehicle where Avery was waiting to pull off, Aayan looked to see if Caze was ok. Looking in the podium area he found Caze standing in the doorway of the Foundation building behind a concrete pillar giving him a sigh of relief.

"Drive Avery Drive!" said Aayan in a manic tone.

"I'm going boss. What's going on out there?"

"I don't know. This is getting out of hand. I have to figure this out. It feels like I am being toyed with. Whoever is doing this could have killed me today."

"You need to get to the root of your truth. That's what I think it is."

"What does that mean?" said Aayan before he was interrupted by the ringing of his phone.

Without haste Aayan answered the phone unaware of who it was. At this point he was just hoping to hear Caze voice on the phone. Instead, it was a voice he recognized but couldn't quite put a face or name to it. The voice had a hint of disgust over top of a very heavy Russian accent.

"You black bastard. You will pay for everything that you have done. You can be touched anywhere, even in that nice cozy one elevator loft you live in. You are not safe. Vengeance will be ours." said the man on the phone.

"WHO IS THIS? WHAT DO YOU WANT FROM ME?" yelled Aayan putting the phone on speaker as he looked at the phone to see if a number appeared.

"You will remember my face when you look me in my eyes while I am cutting your balls off. Ohh and don't worry the number is unknown and untraceable. You will pay one way or the other."

"I don't know you. Do you want money? What do I have to do to make this stop?"

"You can't right the wrongs you have done. You will pay with your life." said the man laughing as he hung up.

"What the fuck Avery. What do I do?"

"Sounds like you need to reconcile your past. It's the only way to resolve this." said Avery as he followed the convoy thru traffic back to Aayan's place.

"Ok?"

"Remember your past will always come back to haunt you."

CHAPTER 16
YURI

Sitting at his desk with a smile on his face staring out of a townhouse window on the second floor, Yuri lit a cigar and took a bump of cocaine before placing the next call. Wiping his nose and snorting really heavy he placed the next phone call.

"The plan is in motion and the call was placed, I'll be awaiting the next instructions." said Yuri.

"I'll let you know when to grab him. We need to be ending this soon. No more games." said the woman on the phone.

"You are the one calling the shots. We could have ended this game today, but you want to make him suffer. Why, I don't know. Whatever he did to you can't be as bad as what he did to me."

"It was worst. Just keep doing your part and this will all work out. The next thing I want you to do is find a way to see him in person when he is with one of his friends. Let him see your face so he can remember you and kill his friend. Can you handle that?"

"No task to tough. Can I wound the black bastard?"

"NO! He is ours. You don't do him any harm besides the harm I tell you too. Do you understand me?"

"Blah, Blah, Blah. Whatever you say!" said Yuri as he hung up the phone.

Yuri looked over at the rustic bookshelf and reached for a picture. The picture was one of the last memories that he had to hold on to. He didn't want to think about that fateful night where everything changed for him. The violent memory of that night replayed over and over when he slept causing him to age like spoiled milk. Taking one more bump of cocaine he stood up and began to stare out the window again, this time deep in thought. He slowly looked over his shoulder at the news showing everything that transpired today and began to laugh out loud.

Staring at the fright on Aayan's face, he paused the TV and garnished a huge smile. The smile was similar to the joker, evil, full of malice and hatred. He walked over to the TV and began to pet Aayan's frozen face on the screen and began to repeat to himself sinisterly.

"I am going to get you soon you black bastard. This is for him!"

Unpausing the TV he fixed a glass of Russian Vodka, took a shot and yelled!

"YOUR DAY IS COMING, YOU BLACK BASTARD! YOUR DAY IS COMING!

CHAPTER 17
FIX IT

Exiting the vehicle in front of Petworth Pharmaceuticals, the security detail surrounded Aayan escorting him to the secure conference room waiting on him. He looked back over his shoulder and yelled for the detail to bring Avery in as well out of fear for his life. The security detail obliged by surrounding him as well and bringing him inside the building which had been heavily secured as if the president was visiting. After the last attack Jason made a call to double the security presence.

Rushing thru the hallway to the elevator Aayan observed the sense of urgency on the face of everyone they passed. They feared for him and everything he had going on. Moving into the elevator the security detail surrounded him to shield him from the glass window. Aayan could feel the warm breath of his security detail all over him and it disgusted him. He was unsure if it was a combination of the men or if one of them had shit chips for lunch. The smell was strong enough for one of the security guards to make a joke about it, but Aayan didn't find it funny.

Pushing his way off the elevator when the door opened, he noticed the army of security standing by the conference room. In the conference room t waiting for Aayan was a Detective, five police officers, Caze, Jason the head of security, Zack, Herb, Byron, Bryan and Buck. He was followed in the room by Avery who was astonished at the site of the room. He looked at the table and rubbed it before he took a seat next to Aayan.

"Guys you are my brain trust. We need to work diligently with the police officers to try and figure this out. There have been repeated attempts on my life. I don't know why, but this last attempt felt like they were toying. with me, I don't like it. I am not a game, and neither is my life." said Aayan banging his fist on the table.

"I'm not gonna lie, today was scary Aayan. I don't know what you did to provoke this, but it needs to be taken care of." said Caze in a concerned tone.

"That's why we are here." said the Detective as he stood.

"I received a phone call from someone who said they know me and that I was going to pay. I have already shared that with the detectives. They are currently running the number to see if they can get a track on it. I need everyone to be safe until we can figure this out."

"It seems like they know your every move Aayan. If they wanted us, they would have had us by now... Just think about it. That's why it's important that we get your paperwork in order, we don't know how this thing is going to pan out." said Zack as he started to look around the room.

"Agreed." said Herb, Caze and Buck simultaneously.

"This is why we have reason to believe this is an inside job and we will be questioning everyone in this room." said the Detective.

"Even me. I'm just the driver." said Avery.

"Everyone. You all have access to his scheduling and daily routines." said the Detective in a smug tone.

"I'm not saying anyone in here is guilty, but I have to take precautions. My life is being threatened and I need all of this fixed. We have to start somewhere and all of you in this room is a start. Please just cooperate and it will be over before you know it. I'm sure you all will breeze right thru the questions. There are no hard feelings. I love all you guys, but this has to be done."

"This is what is about to happen now. We are going to take five of you, place you in individual rooms and you will be questions on the events that have taken place. After questioning if we have no probable cause, you will be brought back to this conference room until we are completely done." said the Detective as he signaled the officers to escort Caze, Buck, Avery, Jason and Herb out of the room.

Sitting in the conference room Aayan rotated his chair to look at the wall and began to think about his past. He thought a lot about the man on the phone call said to him. He started thinking about his past and which part of it was coming back to haunt him. A calm settled over him as he closed his eyes and began to think about everyone he had wronged for survival while he was abducted. The list of people it could be was taller than the old twin towers and at this point he needed a real clue as to what was going on.

Nearly sitting in the room in silence for an hour the five that were escorted out had returned. Zack, Byron and Bryan then left out with the police. Aayan stared at the demeanor of the men as they walked back in and sat down. They all looked irritated and confused.

"Are you guys ok?" said Aayan.

"Yeah, I am fine. They asked me a lot of questions about you. They were inquiring more about how you came into wealth and who you may have crossed to get where you are. Seem like they really didn't care about the attempts on your life." said Caze.

"I felt the same way. It was confusing, it was as if they were coming for you. It felt like being a jury member." said Avery looking around the room for consensus.

"Where did your wealth come from Aayan? It surely was a focal point Batman." said Herb.

"None of that is important Herb. Stay the course we need to figure this out."

"Aayan this is the course. Just making an assessment of the questioning. I think they think you robbed someone or attained your money illegally and that person wants the money back." said Caze.

"I am not a thief! I worked hard for my wealth just like everyone else. That shouldn't even be the focal point of this investigation."

"Well, it is young man. It is… You really need to reconcile with your past if you want this to end." said Avery.

Aayan sat silently looking around the room thinking as Avery's words really began to settle like day old concrete. He began to rub his temple in thought as he always did when he was trying to figure something out. The awkward silence was interrupted by Herb.

"Since we are here let's conduct business." said Herb.

"Yes let's do that." said Aayan.

"We have to get this paperwork signed should anything happen to you Aayan. There would be chaos… You don't have a will, a next of kin and nothing in writing stating who you are turning the company over to. That has to be addressed. We can all sit here and review it once Zack gets back." said Caze.

"That is important, but my job is to make sure it doesn't get that far. We have had to many issues until things calm down, we need to get Mr. Petworth to a safe house away from the madness." said Jason.

"It has gone too far and whose fault is that security man. Yall supposed to be the best in the world. From the outside looking in yall suck. Why he still has this security detail perplexes me." said Caze.

"Sir, I understand there have been holes in our defense. But…," said Jason.

"But what? Yall playing with my life too." said Avery cutting Jason off.

"Services are straight one star garbage. I would not recommend." said Caze as he chuckled looking over at Jason.

"Enough guys. Sitting here going back and forth isn't going to solve anything. What is the plan Jason." said Aayan as he began to massage his temple.

"Sir we have a safe house to take you to. Your home has been compromised. We can't take you upstate because that home may be compromised as well. We are going to take you to undisclosed location in New Jersey as soon as the armored guard arrives." said Jason.

"That sounds like a plan. I need the quiet until I sort this out."

"What sounds like a plan?" said Zack as he walked back in the room and took a seat.

"Batman is about to go into hiding." said Caze making everyone laugh.

"Well even Bruce Wayne took a break from Gotham." said Aayan.

"We need to review the paperwork?" said Zack.

"We will... I am going with him." said Herb and Caze unison.

"Well, I'm the driver so I guess I am going to." said Avery.

"There is one more person that I want to have access to the safe house, my therapist Tamika Siler. I want to continue my therapy sessions."

"Yeah, make sure she comes." said Caze rubbing his hands together.

"Ok sir we will make that happen for you. The detail is here and ready to go. We need to make our way downstairs." said Jason.

"Can I use the bathroom first? You know I'm old and my bladder doesn't work like it used to." said Avery

"Of course." said Aayan as he stood up and looked around the room.

"We can stop on the way to the elevator, but we have to move now so the safe house isn't compromised." said Jason as he walked over towards the door to talk to the security detail.

Everyone stood and started walking towards the door surrounded by security. Byron, Bryan, Buckholt and Zack stood to the side watching the sea of people make their way towards the elevator. Enroute Avery slid thru the crowd of people and eased into the men's bathroom. Hastily, Avery returned from the bathroom to catch up with the crowd. Aayan noticed and commented.

"Damn that was quick. You must have really needed to go."

"When you get up here around this age and your body tells you to go, you go. Hopefully you make it to see this age because most don't. Do you think you are going to make it?"

"I know I will. I just have to make it thru this."

Exiting the elevator at the bottom there was a platoon of armed security guards in military grade gear standing outside. The situation felt safe walking towards the vehicles till one of the security guards walked by lifted his face shield, lowered his mask and smiled at Aayan. Everything slowed down as they made eye contact with each other before, Aayan head was lowered by Jason and he was pushed in the vehicle. Avery hopped in the front and adjusted his seat while looking in the mirrors to see if the army of security hand mounted up yet.

Sitting between two guards with a perplexed look as the convoy rolled out, Aayan thought he was imagining who he just saw and if it was real. If he was hallucinating, he knew he needed his therapy session more than ever. Digging in his pocket he called Tamika.

"Are you ok?" said Tamika in a concerned tone.

"Yeah, I am good. I need a session tomorrow. I will have a team of people pick you up and bring you to my location if you are available."

"Yes, I am available tomorrow. What time?"

"Early as possible, maybe 10am. I think I am seeing things... A guy that I talked about in a session... I think I just saw him."

"Well, Aayan you have been thru a lot. Maybe your mind is trying to rationalize everything by putting a face to it. Let's talk about it in the session tomorrow."

"But Tamika it felt so real, as if he was there."

"OK are you going to call the police?"

"No because I can't tell if it was real or not."

"Ok tell me when we talk tomorrow who you think you saw."

"OK... have a good day, I'll see you tomorrow, Tamika."

Aayan looked up to see Avery staring in the rearview mirror. He began to stare back as if they were in a staring contest. The look in Avery's eyes was different, it was one of confusion, anger and pain. The look in his eyes showed something was on his mind. Aayan had to snap out it with a quirky comment forcing Avery to stop staring.

"Eyes on the road old fella."

"Make a mends young man. Reconcile your past."

CHAPTER 18
RECOVERY

The ride to the safehouse felt like it took forever but it was good for Aayan. He needed the time to clear his mind and think things thru. He started thinking back to the person he seen on the way out of the building. Thinking about it made him sweat profusely. He started thinking about his past and couldn't process having left any loose ends after getting out of Europe.

The safehouse was a huge mansion in the middle of ten acres of land. It was in a gated community, behind an additional gated fence. There were layers of protection that would make it extremely difficult for anybody who tried anything. The scenery was beautiful, trees, lakes and wildlife were everywhere. Pulling up to the house the convoy began to slow.

"Looks like we are stopping at what seems to be home sweet home for the time being boss." said Avery.

"You are welcome to stay if you want." said Aayan.

"No thanks I have to be home later."

Walking in the house Caze, Herb and Aayan found what looked like a panic room with a long conference table. They sat down looked around and decided to conduct business. The future of the business was in limbo if Aayan demise were to come. They had to sort it out.

"Ok this thing is a few hundred pages long." said Caze pulling a big manila folder filled with paperwork out.

"Damn yall want my whole life should something happen to me. Do we have to do this today? I really just want to relax for a little while. Matter of fact guys lets relax. I mean there was just another attempt on my life. Can we do something other than business right now." said Aayan as he stood and walked over to the radio.

"Yes, business is something that we should be handling right now. We can't keep putting this off." said Caze.

"Agreed. We actually have the time now. You are surrounded by an army of security and its quiet here." said Herb.

"Ok that's understandable. Can we get to business tomorrow after my therapy session since you guys are staying out here?"

"I'm not staying. I came for the business. If we aren't conducting business, I am going to have some of your army escort me home." said Herb getting up and walking over to the liquor cabinet to pour three glasses of cognac.

"Well, I'm staying… I have never stayed in a house this big ever. I mean I do work for cheapest billionaire in the world." said Caze as he began to laugh.

"Shut up man. You're staying because Tamika is going to be here tomorrow." said Aayan as he took a glass of cognac from Herb.

"That too. There are more than enough rooms in here." said Caze as everyone began to laugh.

Avery walked in astonished at how huge the house was on the inside. He stared at all the paintings on the walls, the classical dining room set, and the family room with the 100-inch TV mounted on the wall. The sight of this kind of lifestyle made his jaw drop. Stepping into the room where Aayan was sitting with Caze and Herb, he smiled at the men laughing. They reminded him of his youthful days and his son.

"For some guys on the run yall sure are mighty festive." said Avery as he stood in the doorway.

"If I'm going to die, I want to be found with a smile on my face." said Caze.

"That's no way to think at your age young man."

"It is when your boss is Batman." said Herb making the room laugh.

"Boss do you need anything else from me? I am about to head out." said Avery.

"No, I am good. I will see you tomorrow good sir."

"Since we aren't handling business, I think I am going to hop on the convoy out too. said Herb as he finished his drink.

"Ok, you two be safe." said Aayan as he stood to give each of them a handshake.

Walking towards the door the security detail stood outside scattered all over. Avery walked to talk to the security detail while Herb waited in the doorway looking at a painting hanging on the wall. Two members of the security detail walked up to Herb and escorted him to the last vehicle in the convoy. Avery jumped in the vehicle he drove for security, and they drove off. Herb looked out the rearview window at the view of the house getting small and out of sight. He looked down at his phone and started reviewing work emails keeping him occupied during the ride. Looking up and straight ahead he noticed that Avery's vehicle was gone, and he had no idea where he was.

"Guys I think we missed a turn or something."

"We are taking a detour for your safety." said the Driver as he lowered his mask and looked in the rearview mirror.

"What detour is this?" said Herb as he tried to look at a map on his phone to figure out his location

"Sir just relax. You are safe." said the Driver as he reached down to turn on a cellular disabling device installed in the vehicle.

Checking his phone again, he realized he didn't have any service. He tried to make his way to grab the driver without success. He was restrained by the security in the back and had his face covered with a rag soaked in chloroform. Trying to fight the men off Herb passed out. The last thing he saw before he dimmed out was a bag being put over his head.

"You chose the wrong person to work for my friend." said the Driver.

★

After a long night of drinking, Caze and Aayan woke up the next morning to the ring of Aayan's phone. They both sat up rubbing their temples. The security is standing in the hallway like statues staring at the two starting to move around. The ringing of the phone began to echo loudly thru the house. The sun beamed thru the window shining directly into Caze eye as he stood up grabbing the back of his pants.

"What the hell wrong with you man?" said Aayan.

"I had to check to make sure that you aint take no booty… I saw you on the news. They say you a booty warrior." said Caze as he began to yell laughing.

"Shut up."

"You shut up and answer the phone already damn."

Looking down to see who was calling he realized it was Tamika and put the phone on speaker. He looked up at Caze and pointed at the phone. Caze began to jump around dancing like he was having sex with the air. Aayan laughed loudly before taking the call.

"For person who lives in constant danger, you sure are in a good mood. I know if it were me, I would be worried."

"Trust me I am. Is the security there to pick you up for therapy today."

"They just arrived. I just want to make sure we are still good."

"Ok I will see you when you get here. I have a lot to talk about today."

"I'm sure you do. It's time to reconcile your past. "

"I will see you when you get here."

"Man, you gotta let me hit it before you do therapy. She got that fire." said Caze as started massaging his genitals.

"Business first you creep."

"I am trying to give her the business."

"Have you heard from Herb this morning. He usually sends them garbage motivational quotes in the morning." said Aayan looking at his phone.

"Nope, maybe he slept in this morning. He needs it as hard as he been working."

"Yeah, that would make sense, it's been a lot going on. I am about to get in the shower before she gets here. "

"See I'm getting my shower when she gets here. That's the difference between me and you." said Caze as he walked towards the kitchen.

"What you about to make?"

"All the money you paying this security make one of them cook. I am eating cereal, if there is any in this big ass house."

"I'm sure you will figure it out. I'm getting in the shower it won't be long before Tamika gets here."

After taking a long shower to gather his thoughts, Aayan got out of the shower and stared in the mirror as he often does. This time looking in the mirror it felt different. It felt like he were having an outer body experience, as if he was standing over his shoulder looking at himself in the mirror. He was told by a guy a long time ago when you have those kinds of experiences your soul is in danger. Aayan always took that as if it meant the end was near. Getting dressed in clothes that security went to the store and bought while him and Caze were getting drunk, he looked out the bedroom window and stared at the luxurious Olympic size pool in the distance over the tall yard fence. He embraced the sunlight before he was interrupted by Caze yelling.

"Aye fool my boo just pulled up. Bring your ass down here!"

"Shut up man. I am on the way down."

Walking to the base of the stairs he saw Caze heavy in conversation with Tamika. He couldn't make out if she was happy or annoyed. She looked over and gave him a nod to the side as if she was saying let's go get therapy started. Aayan smiled gave a thumb up and intervened.

"Alright, Alright… time to let her do what she came here to do." said Aayan.

"I am fool. What do you think I'm talking about." said Caze.

"How are you doing Aayan? Do you have a certain area you want to do the session today." said Tamika.

"There is a study that is completely private that we can use by the kitchen."

"That sounds perfect. Nice seeing you again Caze. I'll talk to you after this session." said Tamika as she mouthed to Aayan "No, I won't."

"Let's get this therapy started. I have things to say today."

"Good I hope so. I am sure there is a lot you still have to talk about."

CHAPTER 19
LIVE YOUR TRUTH

Getting comfortable in the study Tamika sat down pulled her pen and pad out and stared at Aayan. She looked around at the setting in the room and looked back at him in attempt to gage his temperament. He was fidgeting more than usual. She couldn't tell if it was because of everything going on or if he was hungover from the night before. Watching him sit down on the recliner across from her, she noticed that his foot tapping, and fingernail biting were extremely rapid.

"Aayan slowly count to five. Inhale, exhale and countback down to one." said Tamika as she reached to stop his leg from shaking.

"The man I saw... I am sure he was the driver of the vehicle that I was abducted in. The guy who tried to show remorse for me. The guy whose brother was killed at Randy's order for abusing me."

"Aayan, you have been thru a lot in the last few weeks. Maybe everything that is going is retriggering trauma from your past causing hallucinations. Just a mere figure of your imagination." said Tamika.

"But it felt so real Tamika. I'm sure it was him."

"So, you saw a man from your past on your security detail. I seriously doubt that Aayan, these men are vetted very well."

"Yeah, you're right. I didn't think about that. OK let's get this started."

"Last time we spoke you were in Europe... but you stand before me as a billionaire. Shall we continue there."

"No just understand I did horrible things and people were hurt. I did enough to make the money I needed to make it back to America. The reality is the incident with Julius was just the beginning of the things I had done. I was completely brainwashed. My soul was gone.... I was a robot being controlled by evil people. I was a teenager robbing, killing, raping, being raped and selling drugs. It was horrible. I crossed a lot of people, hence why it's hard to narrow down what's going on." said Aayan as he leaned his head back looking at the ceiling.

"How did you get back?"

"Long story short... I was on a drug deal and things went sour. I walked away with enough money to buy an identity and make it back to America. I flew first class and touched down at BWI airport. I had $12,000, a fake passport, a suitcase filled with socks, underwear and a mind full of ill intentions. Let's start from there... "

"Is this going to lead to Randy?" said Tamika as she took notes."

"It's going to end with Randy." said Aayan while biting his nails.

Getting settled back into life in America, the only thing Aayan had on his mind was revenge. He wouldn't have committed any crimes or suffered the way he did if it wasn't for Randy. He still had a pain in his heart for his mother, but she birthed him, and he was sure he could forgive her, should the opportunity arise. Moving from Motel 6 to Motel 6 communicating with kids who he could tell had been trafficked, he spent months trying to piece together the puzzle of Randy's compound location. Aayan knew it was in the mountains, he just needed to get there. During these months Aayan acquired a car he paid cash for, a trunk full of weapon and niche for learning people. In these months when his money started running low, he resulted to selling small amounts of weed to get the things he needed.

One fortunate day after his persistent search, Aayan went to Target and had a breakthrough in his search. Sitting in the parking lot looking at a map that he marked up during his search, he banged his hands on the steering wheel in anger grabbing the attention of a man in front of the car. They made eye contact and Aayan immediately recognized the man he was looking at. It was one of Randy's security guards. He didn't notice a now nearly 17-year-old Aayan. The things Aayan went thru hardened him emotionally and physically. He looked weathered for his age, a drastic change from his present state.

Throwing the map in the passenger seat Aayan watched the man carefully as he hopped in a white Range Rover. He waited for the man to leave and began to patiently follow. Maintaining a safe distance behind the vehicle the area began to look familiar, the ridgelines, the trees, roads and most importantly the narrow road that led back into the forest. Aayan drove by the entrance looking for a nearby motel. After checking in and waiting for the sun to go down Aayan rolled back down the dirt road slowly with his lights off. Two miles into the dirt road there sat Randy's house. The sight of the house flooded Aayan with an influx of emotions. He was angry, sad, mad, furious and ready at the same time.

An emotion filled Aayan drove slowly around to the top of the ridge and parked. The last time he had been to this spot is when he attempted to run away. The trail to the house was still clear enough to see the cave he hid in. Aayan decided to use the cave as his base of operations for his revenge plot. For months he envisioned this day, it was already planned out. Randy was a creature of habit. Aayan knew Randy hated change so this would make it easy to complete his mission. Checking the day on his watch he knew Randy would be relaxing in the basement where he held his fights, it was his hangout.

Shortly after 1 am Aayan started loading himself down with guns and rifles. In his mind it didn't matter who was there, they were going to die for dealing with such an evil man. Approaching the perimeter of the fence he noticed that there was no security and the house looked as if it didn't have the high maintenance upkeep it had in the past. He began to wonder if it even still belonged to Randy. The hog pen was empty, the grass was long, and the bushes were untrimmed. Aayan slowly eased his way to the dimly lit back porch and began to look around the glass window of the backdoor. He noticed three pictures of Randy hanging on the wall, encouraging him to slowly open the unlocked backdoor.

"Good ole Randy! Still don't believe in locking doors." said Aayan to himself as he tiptoed slowly thru the hall looking around for security.

Just as expected the basement light was on, the door was open, and music was playing. The music was different than the Russian grunge rock he listened to before. He was listening to Beethoven's 'Symphony 5' and that definitely wasn't a Randy thing. He was into everything that was related to drugs, guns and violence. Slowly walking down the steps Aayan noticed fresh crayon drawings on the walls as if Randy received a fresh batch of young children. Slowly peaking around the corner Aayan noticed the throne, but the rest of the basement was different. It was filled with toys, TV's and paintings of cartoon characters. Aayan stood in awe that Randy was stooping to this level to trick kids into his abuse, angering him even more.

Stepping around the corner he saw Randy sitting in a chair under a light. The site of Randy began to infuriate Aayan as he inched closer to him. He looked in front Randy and there was a hospital bed with a woman hooked up to a heart rate monitor and IV. Quietly cocking the 9mm pistol, Aayan put it to Randy's head and shoved it to the side forcing Randy to put his hands up.

"Please don't kill me. I have money. I will tell you where the safe is just let me live." said Randy as he cowered in fear.

"Where is the safe? How much is in it" said Aayan in a muffled voice.

"The safe is behind the throne and there is at least $20 million in there. Please just let me live. I have people that need me. I left it open. I just had to pay someone who went and picked up her prescription."

"Fuck her and fuck you. DO YOU REMEMBER ME?" yelled Aayan shifting himself in front of Randy putting the gun to his forehead.

"You... Aa...." said Randy in disbelief before he was interrupted by Aayan.

"Yeah, asshole it's me, Aayan. Remember me? Do you remember making me fight? Do you remember making me take your special candy? Do you remember shipping me overseas? Everything that happened to me you piece of shit."

"I am not that man anymore. I am sorry."

"You shouldn't have been that man in the first place. You could have taken me home and let me explain everything to my dad. Did you? No! So, fuck your changes."

"Please don't do...." said Randy before he was shot in the head twice by Aayan.

While emptying the clip of the 9mm into Randy head Aayan heard a loud scream.

"DADDY NO. DADDY!" screamed a boy and a girl standing in the doorway.

He continued to pull the trigger listening to the click of the empty gun trying to silence out the screams of the children. He stopped, stared at the kids and walked over to the woman in the bed. Reaching for his 38mm, he stared at the woman and looked back at the children sobbing. He looked back at the woman, looked down at Randy and looked at the kids again.

"Go be with your mother." said Aayan as he walked over to the throne and sat.

"Mommy, Daddy!" yelled the kids in unison as the boy hovered over Randy crying and the daughter hugged her mom.

Aayan sat in the throne and watched the sobbing kids, the bed written mother and Randy laying in a pool of his blood, and brains. He looked behind the throne and realized Randy wasn't lying about the safe being open. It was loaded with money, more than Randy said. The sight made Aayan reflect on all of the pain he had endured over the years, and he knew he had to change. The mission was complete, and it was time for him to go, but he wouldn't leave empty handed. Yelling at the kids to stay in place, Aayan went upstairs grabbed four large suitcases to load all of the money up. After he completed emptying the safe, he threw the kids $10,000.

"Don't spend all of it at once. I would say I am sorry for your dad but I'm not he was a bad man. If I didn't do it someone else would have." said Aayan as he began lugging the suitcases up the stairs.

Aayan loaded the suitcases full of money in a land rover that was parked in front of the house. Pulling off to head back to his car parked on the ridgeline he looked in the rearview mirror and saw the little boy and girl standing on the porch watching him leave. They held each other and stared at Aayan till he wasn't visible anymore.

"So, is that how you came into your wealth?" said Tamika as she reached for her phone.

"It was a start... I made a lot of investments that paid off for me. I got into real estate, music, and I opened a laundromat, but I did it under aliases or other names. After I officially changed my name to Petworth I got into pharmaceuticals and boom here I am." said Aayan looking down at his hands.

"How do you feel about getting revenge on Randy? Do you feel any remorse for what you did?"

"I still felt empty after killing him, but it was something that needed to be done. I would do it again if I had the chance. I have no remorse for taking him away from his family. He didn't care when he took me from mine." said Aayan staring Tamika in her eyes.

"I have to use the restroom. May I be excused Aayan?"

"Sure, it's right next to the kitchen."

"When I get back, I want to talk about the how you felt seeing the kids in pain."

Sitting patiently waiting Aayan began to think about the guy that looked familiar, the kids, Julius, and all the others that were hurt on the path he was put on after he was taken from Kings Dominion. He thought to himself would he have the life he has now? Would he have survived if he stayed in Europe longer? Should he have stayed overseas? In the middle of his thoughts Tamika walked back in and sat.

"So Aayan how do you feel about the kids?"

"At the time I didn't care about those kids. Fuck em. Now I wonder what happened to them, how they turned out and were they safe."

"Do you feel like you did them wrong? What are your feelings about that?"

"I didn't do them wrong. They still had a mother to care for them. I didn't kill her, and I didn't kill them. They got a fair deal out of this situation."

"A fair deal? Aayan, you killed their dad in front of them, and left them with a small amount of money compared to what you took. You don't have any remorse at all for that?" said Tamika as she looked down at her pad.

"I'm not a monster. I do wonder about them, but I have no remorse for killing Randy. He would have got what he deserved no matter who was there." said Aayan as his phone began to ring.

"Do you have any other feelings about this? Anger, fear, frustration, sadness." said Tamika as she continued to take notes.

"I don't feel any of that at the moment, but I have to take this call. Its Herb facetiming me. I haven't heard from him today, so I have to take this." said Aayan as he looked at his phone.

"Ok that's fine. I understand." said Tamika as she pulled her phone out and began to text.

"Wassup Herb? Are you ok? There wasn't a message or call this morning." said Aayan.

"Wassup you black bastard? You remember me? I saw you face to face. I told you... your day is coming... it's coming soon." said Yuri smiling into the camera in the back of a van.

"Where is Herb? What have you done with Herb you bastard?" yelled Aayan as he signaled for Tamika to go get security.

"Ohh this guy. I don't think he is available at the moment please leave message." said Yuri while laughing and flipping the camera to a naked horribly disfigured Herb.

"What do you want please? Please don't hurt him anymore. Do you want money? I'll give you money but please don't hurt him anymore!" screamed Aayan as security, Caze and Tamika came rushing in the door.

"I'll get my just due bastard. This is what I think of your money." said Yuri as he took a dull blade and slowly sliced Herbs throat.

"NO!" yelled Aayan and Caze as they watched Herb squeal like a dying pig.

"Herb made it to work today!" said Yuri as two of the men with him threw Herbs naked, disfigured, bleeding body in front of the Petworth Pharmaceuticals building.

"See you soon!" said Yuri before hanging up.

With tears in his eyes Aayan began to yell at the security detail.

"How the hell could this happen? I knew the detail was compromised!" Get out of my sight all of you. NOW!" yelled Aayan.

"Aayan take a deep breath and calm down." said Tamika

"Fuck calming down you get out too. Caze get us a vehicle so we can go get Herb."

"That's not smart Aayan. I am going to miss Herb too, but that's not smart." said Caze with tears in his eyes.

"JUST DO IT! PLEASE!" yelled Aayan as he stood and hugged Caze sobbing heavily.

"It's going to be alright brother." said Caze while embracing Aayan with a hug.

Tamika walked over and rubbed Aayan on his back. She leaned down, looked him in his eyes and stared.

"It's ok. Let it out Aayan… Let it out…" said Tamika before she was interrupted by her text alerts.

"I got him Tamika. I will arrange for a police escort to take you home. In the meanwhile, Aayan we have to relocate again." said Caze.

"I just want to go home." said Aayan repeatedly as if he was reliving his abduction.

CHAPTER 20
HERB'S FUNERAL

After the events that took place the previous week, Aayan started having dark thoughts. All he thought about was killing the man from his past. He was systematically destroying Aayan. His focus was how he could get ahead of him or catch him. Because of all the things Aayan did in his past he couldn't tell the police where he knew the man from. Aayan knew there weren't statutes of limitations on murder. Taking deep breaths pacing back and forth in the conference room in Petworth Pharmaceutical's under heavy police guard, Aayan turned the TV's on to tune into Herbs funeral virtually.

Caze walked in the conference room, patted Aayan on the back and sat down. Byron, Bryan, Buckholt, Zack and Avery walked in a little after Caze taking seats all around the table in preparation for the funeral. There was an awkward silence in the room. All of the men sat at the table and stared at each other. They felt a pain, a pain so deep with everything going on it made the air in the room thick as strippers at Magic City. Caze had no jokes, the twins had no comments, Avery stared at Aayan and Buckholt had his head down.

"Sorry about all of this gentlemen. I never meant for any of this to happen. There are things from my past that you guys don't know about and it's coming to light. I never wanted to see anyone hurt or killed." said Aayan looking around the room at the sad men.

"Aayan, we have been couped up in this building since we moved last week. My life has completely changed because of some bulshit that you were in. I don't want to die, and I am sure that none of the other guys in here want to die. Whatever you got going on you need to fix it. This is so fucked up. I mean look at us, we can't go home. Aayan dude we can't even go to Herb funeral in person out of fear of another attack. I am angry." said Caze as he stood up and walked to turn another TV on in the conference room.

"I understand your anger Caze." said Aayan before being cut off by Caze loudly.

"Do you! Herb is dead Aayan. We have to have police escorts to go everywhere. Your security detail was infiltrated! How do we know these police aren't on that mans pay roll?" said Caze.

"Sit down Caze. Acting like this not making anything better." said Zack.

"Yeah, it really isn't. Can it at least wait till after the funeral?" said Buckholt as he got up to get water from the minifridge.

"Shut up Buck and give me a damn water." said Caze.

"Anybody else want one."

"I'll take one." said Avery as he got comfortable in his chair.

"Fellas the service about to start." said Aayan.

Sitting the in the conference room staring at the 83-inch TV showing the funeral proceeding, that began with the viewing. Regardless of what was going on with Aayan, Herbs family was there as people walked up and paid their respects. The camera man did a close up on Herb as he laid in his casket at peace. Herb was dressed to impress. The sun shining thru the church windows on Herb made it look like he was in heaven smiling down on the funeral service. The ambience in the church was that of a celebration instead of sadness. The camera man backed his camera off and you could see Herbs family sitting in the front row exchanging conversation. Panning back to the stage the pastor took the mic to let everyone know that the service was beginning in five minutes.

"He looks so at peace." said Buckholt.

"He does. I wish we were there for his family though." said Aayan as he began to tear up.

"It's your fault he is even there. Can we please not talk about wishing we were at his funeral? There shouldn't be a funeral." said Caze while staring at Aayan.

"Ok young man... I understand you are mad but c'mon. What's done is done we can't change it. No sense in steadily poking the bear." said Avery.

"Old man listen this has nothing to do with you. Why are you even here? You didn't know Herb." said Caze.

"He is here because he was invited here. This man has been in the mud with me since all of this started. Now can we please watch the funera, the service is about to begin." said Aayan.

Everyone nodded in agreement. The pastor walked to the podium and opened the service up with a lengthy prayer. The prayer was proceeded with opening remarks and a short video of Herbs life. The video made Aayan cry obsessively, he cried to a point the collar of his shirt soaked. Avery rolled over in his chair, patted Aayan on his back and whispered in his ear.

"Son it will be over with soon. Stay strong." said Avery handing Aayan tissue.

"Thank you, Avery."

After a beautiful hour-long service, the family paid their last respects before the casket was closed. The family was escorted out behind the casket so they could proceed to the Herbs final resting spot at Nat Turner Memorial Cemetery. The family took their time exiting the church because of how close the cemetery was. The cameras in the church stay running as all the men in the conference room watched people hug, shake hands, cry and laugh. Aayan and Caze looked at each other, stood up and hugged. Turning around looking back at the TV, the feed from the church cut off. The two sat back down and an eerie silence took over the conference room before Buckholt broke the silence.

"Herb probably in heaven working on a spreadsheet or a PowerPoint for Gods 3rd quarter budget." said Buckholt making everyone laugh.

"Right." said Aayan and Caze simultaneously.

The feeling of anger and tension began to lighten in the room. The men spent 50 minutes sharing stories about Herb, the good, the bad, the ugly, and the funny. Herb had a way about him that most people liked, and it showed by how many people attended his funeral. The laughter in the room was interrupted by the church camera feed coming back on.

"Why is the feed back on and why is the camera at the gravesite? There is no one there." said Zack pointing at the empty chairs at the cemetary.

"This isn't right. One of you guys go grab the police in the hall and tell them they need to get to the grave site!" yelled Aayan before Yuri popped in front of the camera.

"Well hello friend. How are you doing today? That was a remarkable service wasn't it." said Yuri as he pulled a chair in front of the camera.

"What the hell does he want?" said Caze as all the men in the room stood and stared at the TV.

"Mr. Aayan... I'm sure you know who I am by now. Your good friend Yuri... I'm sure you never knew my name. It wasn't your place to know it. You did know my brother's name though. You do remember V... I'm sure you do... You see I protected you. When he just wanted to hurt you, I protected you. We let you live. You see your friend here is getting a funeral. My brother didn't get a funeral because of you and Randy. My brother was fed to the hogs alive… I can still hear the screams from my brother while I watched you sit in the kitchen and eat like nothing was going on. The pain I felt that day you will feel over and over again till I say it's time for it to end." said Yuri standing up out of the chair and grabbing a small gas can.

"What is he talking about Aayan?" said Caze.

"I want to know what's going on too." said Byron.

"Everyone around you is probably wondering what I'm talking about. You know and I know what I am talking about. Your day is coming. This isn't about money, this isn't about your friends, this is about me and you." said Yuri as he walked over to Herbs casket, opened it, doused Herb in gasoline and set him on fire.

"NOOO!" yelled Aayan watching Herbs corpse burst into flames as Yuri walked back towards the camera.

The police came rushing into the conference room to see all of the men standing and staring at Herbs casket in flames. They immediately dispatched all the police in the area and a fire truck to the gravesite.

"See you soon!" said Yuri before he cut the camera off.

"Aayan what in the fuck were you into?" said Caze.

"It's a long story Caze, but now I have somewhere to start so I can figure this out."

"You better get this shit straight. I don't want to die behind something I didn't have anything to do with." said Caze while beating on the table.

"I'll fix it. I promise that to all of you." said Aayan looking around the room at all of the concerned faces.

"Young man… you have to reconcile your past." said Avery as he leaned over and grabbed a hold of his hand.

"I will. I have no choice in the matter now. I need to figure out how."

CHAPTER 21
ONE MAN'S WEALTH

After three more long days locked down in Petworth Pharmaceuticals the men started becoming weary and wanted to get back to their regular lives. Caze had decided enough was enough and went to Aayan's office. When he got there Zack was already there along with Buckholt. The looks on their face showed the same frustration that Caze felt. He came in sat down and gave a head nod to Aayan.

"Aayan, you didn't tell the police shit, you aren't telling us shit and you sit there like everything is all good. I want to go home without worrying about my damn life." said Buckholt in an aggressive tone.

"You can leave... You see Avery did. I said I am going to fix it and I will Buck."

"He is old, he doesn't care if he dies man. You're playing when this aint a time to be playing." said Buck.

"I agree Aayan. This Batman shit has gone too far. People are really dying out here. What did you do man? Of all the people in the world you can tell us." said Caze.

"See this that bs Aayan. We need to get this paperwork done. I really feel like something may happen to you." said Zack as he looked around the room.

"Agreed." said Caze.

"Everything going on and yall talking to me about some damn paperwork. That damn paperwork can wait. I'm not signing anything or conducting any business till I fix this situation. I lost Herb, I don't want to lose anyone else."

"The paperwork is a safety net in case something does happen to you. Business will run as usual, and people will be left in place. It also will cancel out any notions of a buyout from any other company." said Zack.

"That's all-fine Zack, but I said what I said. Now I have been cooped up in here like you guys. I am frustrated, I am mad about Herb, I am mad at the theatrics of Yuri, I am mad he hasn't been caught but walking around here pissed off wont resolve anything. Matter of fact I will talk to the police and see if they can escort all of us home. I'm tired, yall tired, we all need quiet." said Aayan looking each one the guys in their face.

"I really think we should get this paperwork done Aayan but whatever you say man." said Zack.

"I'm just glad you got rid of that security detail. They were trash. Hopefully none of the police are corrupted because I am leaving." said Caze.

"Leaving to go where." said Avery walking in the door.

"This man running away from business… that's where he is going." said Zack.

"Ohh no you can't do that. Business always come first." said Avery.

"Avery once I get the police escort together, I need you to run me home ok?"

"That's what you pay me for boss. Wherever you need to go."

"Do you know if you die today your business will crumble and there will be no one legally left to run it for you. Is that what you want because you want to go home and hide." said Zack.

"That is messed up Aayan. We have been putting it off for a little while now." said Caze.

"I get it fellas I get it."

"So it's one man's wealth. You made it, and you're going to take it with you." said Caze.

"He gonna leave it to one of those men he touched in DC." said Buck laughing breaking the tension in the room.

"Shut up Buck. You know damn well I didn't do anything to them dudes."

"Man, I don't know. The more this stuff unfolds, the more I realize that I really don't know you at all. I am sure everyone in here can agree with that. I mean you have people trying to kill you about some secret past that you lived, and you are getting accused of rape and murder. I mean c'mon man nothing is too farfetched at this point." said Buckholt as he stood to stretch.

"That's why it's important we get this paperwork done." said Zack.

"It can wait till I get back. Avery lets head to my house please. I want to get a few things that I need. Yall hold tight you know I don't live far from here. I'll be right back."

"We don't know that Batman." said Caze making everyone laugh.

Under heavy police escort Aayan and Avery made their way to their vehicles waiting out front. Traffic was heavy on this rainy morning. Walking outside Aayan noticed that the vehicle was different than his usual truck. He looked at Avery and looked at the car nodding his head in confusion.

"Avery where is the truck?" said Aayan.

"I figured we needed something with a lower profile instead of riding around like the national guard."

"So, you got it approved by the police to drive me around in Toyota Camry?" said Aayan as he stared at the small burgundy car.

"They thought it was a good idea. Their cars are unmarked. Who is going to be looking for you in a 2015 Toyota Camry. All that money you got, they will be looking for the big balling truck in a convoy of cars."

"You are wise beyond your years Avery. That's why I trust you so much."

"Young man… get your tail in this car so we can get to your place."

Getting comfortable in the backseat of the car, Aayan looked around at the clean condition it was in. He looked over Avery shoulder at picture of him and his wife on the dash next to the speedometer. Seeing that picture there brought a calm over him that made him sink into the seat even further. Looking out the window as the line of vehicles began to take off Aayan closed his eyes to get his thoughts together.

"Mr. Petworth would you like some water? I have some bottles of Evian sitting up here in the front." said Avery passing a water to the back.

"Well since you are forcing it on me, I guess I don't have a choice." said Aayan as he opened the water and drank it halfway down.

"Remember I told you I had a son you remind me of… I think it's time I told you the story of my son."

"Do we have enough time?" said Aayan chuckling loudly.

"We have time. Trust me." said Avery as he looked in the rearview mirror to see the same style of Toyota Camry pull behind him.

"Let me hear it…" said Aayan as he began to rub his head and eyes.

"In due time." said Avery as he sped up and swapped positions in the convoy with the burgundy Toyota Camry that was following him.

"What are you doing Avery? Where are we......" said Aayan before passing out in the back seat

"We are going somewhere so I can tell you about my son." said Avery as he turned to head for I95.

With no complications in the vehicle swap Avery escorted Aayan to reconcile his past. This would be the last day Aayan was seen in public.

CHAPTER 22
AVERY

Walking in the door of his home Avery hung his hat on the coat rack next to the door. He closed his eyes and took in the scent of the homecooked meal that he had grown accustomed to receiving when he returned from work. Slowly walking down, the hall touching paintings of his family that hung on both sides of the wall he stopped at the last one just before the kitchen, took it off the wall, kissed it and hung it back up.

"This is for you. It's almost done." said Avery as he hung the picture back up.

Standing in the doorway of the kitchen, Avery admired his wife while she watched the news. The steam from the pots on the oven shifted her attention forcing her to make eye contact with Avery. He walked over, pulled the chair out, and watched Mabel Jean stir the big pot of greens. She looked over her shoulder and cleared her throat.

"How was your day today honey?" said Mabel Jean.

"It was busy to say the least." said Avery while rubbing his hand with his thumbnail.

"Well, I am glad you are safe. When is this going to be over? You keep going to this job, for what I don't know."

"Baby you know I am working on it. You know I am."

"I know you working on it. I just want it all over with. I'm tired of everything going on. It's time to hang it up." said Mabel Jean as she sat down at the table next to Avery.

"Baby, listen it's all going down in a big way tomorrow. Just bear with me."

"I want vengeance Avery and I want it now. The game is over with. Those two men you been dealing with have been calling asking about money that is owed to them. Just figure it out, I am tired of all of this."

"The end is near baby. Now fix me some of them greens before I lose my mind in here woman." said Avery as he tapped on the table.

Walking over to the picture on the wall, Mabel Jean looked over at her shoulder at Avery and began to cry loudly. She stood looking at the picture with her arms crossed. Avery walked over to console her wiping tears from her eyes. He stared at the picture on the wall, reached to take it down, but was stopped as Mabel pulled his hand back.

"Don't take it down. He is where he is supposed to be, hanging next to Jesus." said Mabel Jean as she put her head on Avery shoulder.

"I know baby. He is in heaven with the angels. As old as we are we will be with him soon." said Avery trying to brighten the mood.

"You going to be there with him soon if you don't give me what I want." said Mabel Jean in a stern tone.

"This is a team effort. I am doing all that I can...." said Avery before he was cut off by Mabel Jean.

"Try harder! It took us all of those years to do something that every medical professional said we couldn't do Avery! We conceived a child, a whole child. Our little boy, our sunshine, our everything."

"I know baby I was the one there with you trying. I can't say I didn't enjoy all the trying. Once we got that positive test it was the best thing in the world."

"For me as well. You know this... I also remember the pain of him being abducted from the playground. I remember all the years you spent traveling looking for him and I remember how you found our precious boy Avery.

Unrecognizable, a John Doe, a disfigured corpse. I don't want to hear anymore excuses from you Avery. You know what the hell needs to be done." said Mabel Jean as she walked back into the kitchen.

"Baby..." said Avery before he was cut off again.

"They found him in an alley Avery. They found our boy in an alley in a foreign country. Our sweet boy. Do you remember all the hell you went thru to find out how it happened?"

"You know I do." said Avery as he stared down at his plate of food.

"Fix this or I am done. I am done, do you hear me. After you eat you can make yourself comfortable on the sofa."

"I love you Mabel Jean. It will be done I promise."

"For the sake of our sweet boy it better be. Now eat." said Mabel Jean as she walked out the kitchen.

"I will. You make sure that you are gone to the spot I told you to go to before 10am." said Avery.

"Don't worry about me! Do your part!" yelled Mabel Jean as she walked up the stairs.

CHAPTER 23 BLACK BASTARD

Speeding towards the freeway, Avery drove until he found a rest stop with a fairly empty parking lot. He parked in the back corner under some trees, went to his trunk, tied Aayan up and gagged his mouth. Laying Aayan across the back seat Avery stared at his unconscious body before closing the door. Driving away to make it to the final stop he kept repeating to himself the entirety of the ride. "I don't want to hurt you.. I don't want you to die. I just want my just due." He repeated this over and over again.

Driving in the slow lane down I95, Avery turned on the radio to hear breaking news of the kidnapping of Aayan Petworth, and the description of the vehicle. Avery predicted that and swapped his tags at the rest stop. He knew there was a frenzy to find Aayan, but he stayed the course all the way till they got to Delaware. Merging off of the exit Avery looked in the rear-view mirror and noticed that Aayan was starting to awaken.

"We are almost their young man. It will be over with soon. Just listen and do what you have to do, and you will be home before you know it." said Avery loudly over Aayan muffled yelling.

"Why are you doing this to me?" said Aayan muffled thru the gag.

"What's that young man?"

"WHY ARE YOU DOING THIS!" yelled Aayan thru the gag.

Slowly pulling into the parking lot of an abandoned warehouse, Avery got out of the vehicle and opened the big warehouse door. Driving inside Aayan began to look around and started sweating profusely. The sight of the inside of the building resembled that of which he met Julius. Avery looked in the backseat at Aayan and stared.

"If I ungag your mouth, will you stay silent? I mean if you don't no one is going to hear you out here. We have time to burn before the others get here." said Avery watching Aayan nod up and down.

Ungagging his mouth, Avery and Aayan sat and stared at each other. They both sat speechless. Lost for words Aayan looked around the building thru the window and noticed a lone chair sitting in the middle. The rain drops falling thru the holes in the rusted roof became deafening over the silence. The sound of traffic in the distance sounded like roaring thunder in Aayan's ears.

"Why are you doing this to me Avery. Everything we have been thru, all the good days, good music and funny conversations. What brought you to this point with me? Is it money, I can give you money? What is it?" said Aayan as he sunk down into the back seat.

"I'm not sure what issues the others have with you, well Yuri we know about his brother, but the others I don't know what their qualm is with you."

"Others?" said Aayan.

"Yes others." said Avery.

"What did I do to you Avery?"

"Julius…. Aayan, you did Julius…" said Avery as he began to tear up.

"Julius! My kidnapped kinfolk." said Aayan with wide eyes.

"Don't say his name, you don't know him."

"I do! He was my best friend. While we were overseas, we were stuck together in this room with a TV being controlled…" said Aayan before he was cut off.

"Shut the hell up! They found my sons disfigured body in an alley behind a dumpster. Do you know I was searching all over Europe for him and when I finally got a lead on him it was for being a John Doe at a morgue?

Luckily, I got there on time. They were about to cremate him like they do all the underage John Doe's. This is what it's about Aayan! Redemption, and you are the last part of that." said Avery wiping tears from his eyes.

"Avery, Julius...." said Aayan before he was cut off again by Avery.

"Don't say his name. I will not say it again."

"He was my friend Avery. We were friends. The people there did something to me. I couldn't control anything. I am sorry, I really am. I always wondered what happened to him after that day. I am not the one to blame for this." said Aayan.

"He died by your hand Aayan. I know you weren't the only person behind this. I stayed in Europe moving in dark circles till I found who had my boy. Aayan, I made them pay... I found them and I made them pay. I killed them all and that's what lead me to you. When I found the headquarters, I found the video tape collections that those evil men kept, and I watched them. I watched all the rape, murder, drug abuse and physical abuse. After hours of watching video tapes, I finally came across the video."

"I'm sorry Avery."

"Let me finish... I came across the video of you killing my precious little boy. I watched that video over and over again in tears. I watched it till I could no longer cry Aayan. It was the most painful day in my life."

"I'm really sorry."

"I'm sorry isn't going to cut it. You are indebted to me. The only reason you are still alive is because I started to like you and Madam B has a plan. She is the real mastermind behind everything. She ensured everyone was in place. She knew a lot about you and put all of us together to reconcile your past."

"Avery we could have talked this out. I didn't have to come to this. I am sure we can come up with a better resolution than this. I would have taken care of your family forever." said Aayan as he laid his head on the car window.

"I don't want your money, but I do have to pay Mr. Love and Mr. Reed for their services."

"You set that up! I don't understand why you would do that."

"Because I wanted you to start feeling pain. I wanted you to get a taste of what it feels like to have your livelihood change. Do you think my wife looked at me the same after I let our son get killed? I am the protector of the house and I failed." said Avery looking at the rearview mirror as three trucks pulled in.

"Please Avery. Just let me go free. You will be free soon enough. There is business that needs to be handled. said Avery as he exited the car to greet the vehicle that just arrived.

Trying to look at the people who were exiting the vehicles Aayan was blinded by the LED lights of the front truck. He watched as shadows of people began to emerge from the vehicles. Unknowing of what was to come Aayan began to kick the doors and windows of the car and yell for help. His screams for help went unheard as the door opened. Avery and a man in all black reached in the car and pulled a combative Aayan out on to the hard cold ground. He rolled over and there stood Zack,Tamika and Yuri. With a perplexed look on his face Aayan stared in disbelief.

"Why are you doing this to me? I trusted all of you."

"String him up." said Tamika signaling two of the armed men with them.

"Tie his ass up tight to." said Yuri as he kicked Aayan in the side.

"There has to be another way we can handle this." said Aayan.

"I'm tired of hearing him speak, handle it." said Yuri signaling a man with a rifle to knock Aayan out.

"Man, you don't have to do all that. He is tied up and not bothering anyone." said Avery.

"You handle business how you how handle business and I will handle mine like me old man." said Yuri.

"When is Madam B going to be here." said Zack.

"Shortly she said. In the meanwhile, let's go have a chat with our friend." said Tamika as she walked towards her truck to grab a bag.

"Ok, Ok… if we must. I just want to get this over with so we can go." said Zack.

Tamika and Zack walked away conversing with each other, Avery walked in the office with the busted windows and sat down and Yuri leaned up against his truck watching the Manchester United soccer game. They all had one thing in common they were all there for Aayan. It was just a matter of what they all wanted.

CHAPTER 24
TORTURE

Dragging Aayan across the floor to a beam that ran across the empty bay area, they hung him by his hands to a point where his feet barely touched the ground. He hung there in disbelief and again began to yell for help. His screams went unheard. He tried to spin around to see what everyone was doing with no success. Looking up at the sky he yelled for help once more.

"Help! Help!" yelled Yuri echoing Aayan.

"Let me go. I did nothing to you. That was Randy's doing." said Aayan.

"Don't you dare speak our fathers name. You have no right." said Tamika as she walked out and pulled a chair in front of a dangling Aayan.

"Yeah, our father." said Zack as he walked around, reached in the bag Tamika had and threw $10,000 at Aayan.

"You remember us don't you. Of course you do.... the night at the house... our dad dead in the floor... our mom on her death bed." said Tamika reaching in the bag and grabbing a picture of their mothers' grave site.

"I didn't know he had a family until I got there, and it was too late. Tamika, Zack listen your father was a horrible man. I did what needed to be done......" said Aayan before he was cut off by an angry Zack.

"Who the fuck made you judge, jury and executioner. People change Aayan... Our father changed he wasn't living that life anymore. He was a good man and a great father till you took him away from us. He was keeping our mother alive." said Zack.

"Do you see this Aayan? A few months after you killed our father, our mother passed away. There was no money to maintain the treatment. You took it all. You left two school age children with $10,000, no parents and nowhere to go. Do you understand what we went thru? We

235

didn't know any family. All the family we knew died in that house. Not knowing what to do we, sat in the house with a dead body and a sick mother. My mother wasn't moved to a hospital and our father wasn't taken care of until his faithful security guard friend came to drop the weekly medicine off. We were taken into foster care Aayan. Do you know what that system is like?" said Tamika sliding the picture to Aayan's feet.

"I can only imagine what yall went thru in foster care, but do you understand where your father sent me. It was hell."

"We lived in hell Aayan. I don't care what you went thru. We didn't kill your parents. I held onto that $10,000 waiting for the day to see you face to face again. said Zack looking behind Aayan to see Avery over there listening to the conversation.

"The Randy you knew and the Randy we knew were two different people Aayan. I have hated you for years." said Tamika as she stood up and smacked Aayan.

"Randy? Did I hear this right? You are the offspring of that fucker Randy." said Yuri standing on the wall by the office door.

"Fuck you Yuri." said Zack.

"This is perfect, I am working with that assholes kids. Now I know and knowing is half the battle." said Yuri lighting a cigar.

Tamika looked down at her phone and read the text message and smiled. She picked up the photo, the money and proceeded to walk towards the office followed by Zack and Avery. She looked back over her shoulder and smirked at Aayan.

"We aren't done talking yet." said Tamika.

"Please let's finish talking. I am sorry Tamika; I am sorry Zack." said Aayan as he watched them congregate in the office.

Everyone went in the office except for Yuri. He stayed where he was smoking a cigar and humming here comes the bride over and over again. The humming was annoying everyone, and he didn't care. He just smiled, smoked and hummed. Finally, Zack had enough. He stepped out the office nicely and asked him to stop.

"Do you think I am going to listen to anything one of Randy's children has to say to me. If I knew you were his kids, I would have………." said Yuri before Tamika walked out the door and shot him in the head with a 9mm twice.

"Why did you do that?" said Avery watching Yuri's lifeless body on the ground.

"He was a wild cannon and a loose end. He would have tried to kill me and Zack because of what our father did to his brother. Also, he was going against the grain. The funeral was not part of the plan." said Tamika wiping the blood off of her face with a little towel she had in her bag.

Yuri teeth began to chatter as if he were freezing cold and his body let out a loud moan before he completely stopped moving. Everybody took one last look at Yuri and shifted their focus back to Aayan. With everything that has transpired over the years in Zack, Tamika and Avery's life to them Yuri was just another dead body. Tamika took a seat back in front of Aayan and stared at him. She signaled one of the armed men to cut his shirt off.

"If you move, I will cut you. This razor is sharp." said the guard.

"Please cut me down." said Aayan pleading with the guard.

"Hit him till his ribs bruise." said Tamika sitting back in the chair watching.

Aayan screamed in agony as the guard began to wail on his body like a heavy bag. The screams echoed thru the building like they were in an empty arena. With every blow to the body Aayan began to see stars and dim out from the impact. Right before passing out, he threw up forcing the guard to stop.

"Wake him up." said Tamika.

The guard took the tip of the razor blade and cut Aayan's cheeks sending instant pain thru his body waking him up immediately. The guard then punch him in the opposite cheek knocking one of his teeth out. With blood coming from his mouth Aayan lifted his head and looked at a laughing Tamika and Zack. In the background Avery leaned against the wall trying not to look.

"What do you want from me?" said Aayan spitting blood out of his mouth.

"You stole from us. You took everything. All you had to do was sign the paperwork that needed to be signed and we wouldn't be here Aayan, but no you had to keep putting off and putting it off. I think it's a consensus that we would have all been satisfied seeing you broke and without. Me and my sister were broken and without." said Zack pacing back and forth.

"Yall want my wealth...." said Aayan before he was cut off.

"It's not your wealth, you stole it." said Zack as he reached in the bag to pull out a packet of paperwork.

"How do I know if I sign it that I will be freed."

"That's not up to us, that's up to Madam B. She will determine what happens after you sign it." said Zack.

"If it were up to me, you would face the same fate as our father." said Tamika twirling the gun on her finger and pointing it at Aayan.

"I think he should sis."

"Why don't yall just leave the boy alone. He gets the point. If you are going to kill him get it over with, but we know that's not happening. Just let him be." said Avery as he walked back in the office.

"Fuck that old man. He took everything from us. Do you know the things me and my sister had to do to get in the positions that we are in. Do you think it was easy? We put ourselves thru school, we had no family, at times we were homeless, we had nothing just us. With our wealth we would have been good." said Zack.

"Sound like spoiled white kids issues to me. I see the similar struggle in the hood every day. Please sit your entitled ass down till Madam B get here." said Avery.

"She is almost here." said Tamika while looking at her text messages.

"Please just let me go. I won't go to the police I promise." said Aayan.

Tamika looked at the guard and signaled for another one to come over to Aayan. She looked at them and then looked at him, smiled and told the men to go to work. The two men began to pummel Aayan, breaking his ribs and blacking his eyes. The immense pain from the repeated blows made Aayan pass out again. With joyful cheer, Zack and Tamika applauded the men and their efforts before telling them to stop. Tamika stood caressed Aayan's bloody face, smacked him and walked towards the office. Zack followed behind her. They sat and casually conversed until a guard notified them that a car had pulled up.

"Showtime!" said Zack clapping his hands loudly.

Avery not as excited as everyone else pulled a picture of Julius out of his pocket and began to stroke it with his thumb. He slowly stood and faced away so he could wipe a tear from his eye.

"Let's go old man!" yelled Zack from the office doorway.

CHAPTER 25
MADAM B

Stepping over Yuri's dead body, Madam B stopped and stared at a battered, unconscious Aayan hanging by his hands. She looked over at Tamiika, Avery and Zack and signaled for them to come out of the office. In disgust she looked at them, looked at him and began to tap her foot in annoyance. Madam B is an older black woman that has a low tolerance for failure and bulshit. She had been like that since the early 90's. She didn't play then, and she didn't intend to start playing now.

"Yall did all of this to him and you still couldn't get him to sign the damn paperwork." said Madam B.

"We were waiting on you. That was just for shits and giggles." said Zack.

"Why is Yuri dead?" said Madam B as she tapped her foot.

"He was a loose end that needed to be tied up." said Tamika as she kicked his dead body.

"Well, that's none of my business. Where is the paperwork?" said Madam B.

"It's right here." said Tamika.

"There aint no funny business in this paperwork is it. I had you add the modifications that needed to be added Zack. We don't need any hiccups in the plan unless you are on a mission to be someone's bitch in prison. Now we don't want that do we?" said Madam B.

"No…" said Zack before he was cut off by Madam B.

"DO WE!" yelled Madam B as she grabbed Zack by the cheeks.

"Momma…. Is that you?" said Aayan as he tried to lift his head to look thru his swollen eyes.

Everyone in the room grew so silent that you could hear the rainfall hitting the ground. A state of confusion took over as everyone began to look around at each other. Avery looked back and forth between Aayan and Madam B. So did Zack and Tamika.

"Momma I know that's you. I could never forget your voice. Are you here to rescue me?" said Aayan.

"Hello Son..." said Madam B.

"Son!" said Avery, Tamika and Zack in unison.

"Yes, this is my son!"

"You are Sheka King!" said Tamika in awe.

"Madam B to you young lady."

"Oh, this is cold blooded. I am glad you aren't my mom." said Zack walking over and staring Aayan in the face.

"Momma, are you in on this? Why are you doing this to me?"

"Son all of this could have been avoided if you had just signed the paperwork relinquishing all of your assets over. Look around this room you owe everyone in here. You killed their father. You killed his son. You stole my perfect life." said Sheka as she walked over and stood in front of Aayan.

"Momma if you knew I was alive... why didn't you reach out?" said Aayan as he began to tear up.

"Why didn't you reach out Mr. Billionaire. The first time I saw you on tv, I started doing research on you. I enjoyed trying to find out your background and I must say son its dark. I found out a lot about you."

"If it's money you want, I can give you that."

"Son you have been back for a while. Do you honestly think I wouldn't notice my first child when I saw him? I remember the first time I recognized you. It was at the Walmart in the grocery section. You were following me and your father. I noticed he didn't."

"If you knew it was me, why didn't you call for me?" said Aayan in tears.

"Why would I? You could have approached, and you didn't."

"Does daddy know about any of this? Was he in on getting me abducted?"

"Son, he had no clue how bad I really wanted you gone. He still doesn't know that you are alive."

"Enough of the family reunion shit can we please get on with it. Have him sign the paperwork so we can go." said Zack rolling his eyes like a little kid.

"Momma, Zack, Tamika, Avery… Especially you Avery, I trusted all of you and this is what I get. If yall want my wealth you can have it. I will sign the paperwork, just let me go. I promise I won't say anything. Please just let me go." said Aayan in a quivering voice.

"Oh it's not that simple my friend. There has to be a penalty for your action. Cause and Effect." said Zack.

"Where is the paperwork?" said Aayan.

"Lower him." said Sheka

Lowering Aayan down he collapsed to the floor. His body was weak from the beating, lack of food and water. He crawled over to Sheka's feet and began to plea with her, but the pleas went unheard. He looked around the room and put his head on the ground letting out a long loud cry asking why. Avery walked away to sit in the car. He couldn't take the crying. The sobbing was starting to touch a soft spot in him.

"Why the name Madam B? I want to know before I sign anything." said Aayan.

"Son my middle name begins with a B, you don't remember that...of course you remember that. It's also fitting because I am about to become Madam Billionaire." said Sheka as she slid the paperwork in front of Aayan.

He looked at her, wiped the blood from his mouth and signed the paperwork. Aayan slammed the pen down and laid down flat on the floor for brief moment. The two men that were beating him mercilessly grabbed him and hung him back up. Aayan lifted his head and began to cry at the sight of excitement from Sheka, Zack and Tamika. He heard Avery from behind him walking over towards the trio.

"Are we don't yet?" said Avery in a cavalier tone.

"Not yet. There is one more thing to do." said Zack pulling a Swiss blade out of his pocket and walking towards Aayan.

"No! If it's gonna be done, let me do it." said Sheka taking the blade from Zack.

"Momma no... please no... No, No, No, no... Momma please." said Aayan as Sheka stood in front of him.

"I guess this is goodbye for good son." said Sheka as she raised the blade and slowly ran it across Aayan's throat with no remorse.

"No...MOmmm...noooo......." said Aayan gurgling blood.

"Oh, you are a cruel bitch." said Zack reaching to take the knife back, wiping the blood off on Aayan's pants.

Aayan began to choke and squeal like a pig as all of the blood in his body began to run out like a waterfall. His squirming and squealing made Sheka turn away and cover her ears. They all walked away while he was leaking out and Sheka gave specific instructions on how everything was going to be dispersed and when. Leaving from the scene Zack walked over to Aayan's dead body and patted him on the back.

"Thank you for your contribution kind sir."

"Stop being a dick and come on." said Tamika.

Sheka took one last glimpse at Aayan and knew that this would not come back to haunt her. She had everything planned out from beginning to end. All of the people were strategically picked, the location for the attacks, the location to finish the job, even the day they we going to complete it. She was the mastermind behind everything. She finally reconciled her past and it was like a weight lifted off of her shoulders.

CHAPTER 26
CLOSURE

Months after brutally executing Aayan and taking control of his assets, Sheka began to distribute to all that were involved as promised. She split $20 billion of assets, stocks, properties between Avery, Zack, Tamika and herself. There was a legal clash with Caze and Buckholt trying to take control of Aayan's assets after his disappearance, but it all failed because of lack of sufficient documentation leaving soul responsibility of Aayan estate to Sheka.

That fateful night she made Aayan sign that paperwork leaving her everything, Sheka already paid off a legal team to backdate all of the notary and processing paperwork to ensure she couldn't be traced to the disappearance of Aayan. Things had come full circle for Sheka, she finally got rid of the child she never wanted, her and Keith were financially well off and the kids she had after Aayan had no worries. The days were peaceful till Keith started asking questions about all of the money. She knew that she couldn't keep the money portion secret for long. The media was going to expose her as the new CEO of Petworth Pharmaceuticals. To lessen the blow of the news she decided to take Keith on a vacation to break the news to him.

Walking in the house she hollered for Keith to come to meet her in the kitchen to discuss going on a trip. She knew he was home because his vehicle was in the driveway. He usually met her at the door with a kiss when she returned. This is something he had done since they were young even if they were only separated for ten minutes. On this day he wasn't there to greet her, so she thought he was taking a nap. They were more common in his older age. She walked in the kitchen, fixed a glass of water and sat down at the table. She looked around the kitchen and smiled. She knew that her whole lifestyle was about to change.

After finishing her water, she went to the living room sat down on her favorite recliner and turned the TV on. She began to rock in her recliner with glee before looking at the end table. On the end table there was an open letter. The letter was handwritten, and the envelope was addressed to Keith with a return address that said from Your First Born. This peaked Sheka curiosity making her read the letter.

Dear Dad,

How has life been dad. I have spent a lot of years thinking about how you and Ma were doing. Well, you more than her. She is the reason for my abduction from Kings Dominion. She worked out some deal with Mr. Witt and that went sour. That was the first stop in my wild journey. I have been thru a lot dad, only if you knew. The thing with Mr. Witt went sideways because mom refused to pay and told them to keep me. I don't know if you are aware of this, but I hope you aren't. It would crush my soul if you had something to do with this as well. Anyway, I got dropped off at a place where I had to fight kids to the death. that was before I was shipped overseas for disobeying my owner at the time Randy.

Once I got overseas it was mayhem. I raped and was raped repeatedly. I was forced to use and sell drugs. I committed murder numerous times. I robbed, I stole, I SURVIVED dad. When I say life was a living hell, it was. Can you imagine these things as a young boy? I couldn't but it happened. Dad when did you quit searching for me? How long did you search? I am in therapy now and I felt it was time to communicate with you. I am not prepared to do it face to face yet, but this is a start.

I am doing good right now if you want to know. You have probably seen me on TV... Aayan Petworth. Yeah, it's me dad. I just changed the last name. I'm sure you looked at the TV and wondered if I was your son. I mean we look just alike. With me being a billionaire, I knew you couldn't just pop up and ask, so I am letting you know... yes, it is me your first-born son. Once I got to America and accumulated wealth, I started keeping tabs on you and momma. I wanted to see how yall were *living. I wanted to know if yall were better off without me. I still don't know the answer to that question. Hopefully one day I will muster the courage to find out.*

Anyway, Dad I love you and regardless of what Momma has done I love her too. Hopefully one day we can sit down, and I can get some real answers. Stay positive and again I love yall.

Aayan King

PS: Don't believe the news. I didn't do any of that stuff they said I did. It's all a lie. I won't lie to you.

The letter made Sheka tear up as she crumbled the paper against her heart. The toll of the letter was devastating. Sheka lowered her head and began to ask herself why repeatedly before Keith walked in the room.

"It's a heartbreaking letter isn't it Sheka?" said Keith standing there with a knife in his hand.

"Baby I can explain. Please just let me explain."

"Explain what Sheka. Aayan went thru hell, and he is dead now. Did you have anything to do with his death? Is this where all that money been coming from?" yelled Keith pacing back and forth in the doorway.

"Well baby." said Sheka before she was cut off by Keith.

"Well what Sheka! I received that letter a few days after the first attempt on his life outside of NYC. I sat around contemplating whether I should open this letter or should I throw it away!" yelled Keith.

"I didn't want things to turn out the way they did. I just wanted the problem to go away."

"What problem Sheka. He wasn't bothering us! So, you killed him! You killed my son. That's where this money is coming from. You killed my son! I am glad I read that letter, it was the peace I needed." said Keith dropping the knife in the floor.

"You know how I felt during the pregnancy. I had to do something. I was scared he was going to tell the police about what happened."

"After all these years if he was going to do to it, he would have done it Sheka." said Keith as he walked toward her.

"Are you going to call the police?"

"You don't deserve jail." said Keith as he began to strangle Sheka lifting her out the recliner with a strength he had not felt in years.

Sheka began to gasp for air as Keith grip grew tighter on her neck forcing her body to go limp. Collapsing to the floor she began to dim out from the choke. The grip he had on her neck was beyond removal at this point, so she stopped fighting. She laid there till the white of her eyes turned red and took her last breath. After she died, out anger Keith continued to choke her dead body with tears in his eyes.

Standing over her body he stared in disgust before going upstairs and looking in the locked filing cabinet in her newly formed office room. She kept the lock to that filing cabinet on her person at all times and he never questioned it. Looking in the filing cabinet he found the plans for Aayan from his return to his death if he didn't comply. He closed the filing cabinet went back downstairs looked at Sheka's body one more time.

"Now there is closure. For us and our Black Bastard."

EPILOGUE

Avery

A few days after the assets were distributed Avery still had no closure the way he felt he deserved. The money was a plus, but it didn't bring Julius back. His bloodline ended when he died, and it disgusted him. He knew that Randy had sent his son overseas the same way he sent Aayan. There was no real closure because Aayan had beat him to killing Randy. Still in pursuit of closure he visited Tamika and Zack while they were on vacation in Egypt and killed them both. He electrocuted Tamika in the hot tub in her suite and threw Zack off of his balcony after poisoning his drink. Their deaths ended Randy's living blood line giving Avery real closure. Avery and Mabel Jean never touched the assets that they received from Sheka, they instead adopted a 12-year-old son Lincoln and ensured that on his 18th birthday everything would be transferred to him.

Keith

Immediately after the incident Keith gathered and reviewed the legal documentation and went to the post office. He then went back home to shower and think. After sitting in the house for a couple of days with Sheka's dead body in the floor, Keith went upstairs into the closet and grabbed one of the best dresses she owned as if he was preparing her for a funeral. After getting her dressed Keith took her body to the scene where Aayan was killed, tied her to a chair in the middle of the building and put the plan to get Aayan's wealth in her lap. 24 hours later he made an anonymous call to the police stating there was a dead body in the warehouse. The police arrived and found Sheka's body and the plan. After confirming her identity, the authorities went to notify Keith. Upon arrival to the residence the police found the front door open. Inside they found Keith hanging from the upstairs banister.

Caze

Caze was sitting in his apartment watching CNN and waiting for his lawyer to contact him about the anonymous person that was taking over Petworth Pharmaceuticals. He knew it was a female, but she had her lawyers representing her in court. Sitting in anguish he thought about Aayan and the times they had, and it made him tear up. A knock on the door interrupted him reminiscing about Aayan. There was a mail man at the door with a certified package. He signed for it, walked in sat down and opened it. It was notarized legal documents turning over ownership of Petworth Pharmaceuticals to him. At the bottom of the document, it was signed by Sheka King and notarized and witnessed by Keith King.

Aayan

He matched me... Height, weight, look... everything... He got it, well he had it. Too bad he missed out on Tamika! I knew he was gonna sit and listen to my story... It was sad and I knew no one would. May he rest in peace... dammit... may he Rest In Peace... Anyway....Caze family is good... I'm good.. I cant believe my own damn mother would do this.Im going to burn Avery's house down as soon as I find him. When you have enough money people will do whatever it takes. Me and Caze switched identities... If you haven't figured that out already. I didn't think it was going to go this far... but it did! My closet is cleaned out and I'm here still the CEO of my company.

ABOUT THE AUTHOR

Diya F. Shakoor was born in raised in Landover, Maryland and currently resides in Richmond, Virginia. He is the owner of Hard 2 Oppose Publishing LLC. He is a retired US Army Warrant Officer with multiple combat tours overseas. He has been a lifelong writer of songs, poetry and stories. He challenged himself by entering the realm of writing fiction novels, with this being his first.

Diya is the eldest of nine kids, seven boys and two girls. He is also the proud father of two children. You can find out more about this author and his books on his website (www.authordshakoor.com), Instagram (@theauthordiyashakoor), Twitter (@writingbamma), Fanbase (AuthorDShakoor) and Facebook.com/Diya Shakoor.

Coming Soon: The Grand Scheme of Life 2 (Shabazz), Top Tier Toxicity, Not My Earth, When is He Coming Home, Don't trust what you can't touch Volume 1: Dangerous Paths and Volume 2: Lifelong Punishment, A self-help book for veterans 'The Session Never Ends Once the Rotation Begins' and an autobiography named 'The Infamous Life of a (No) body'.

Made in the USA
Middletown, DE
24 June 2022